THE LAST SAFE HOUSE

A STORY OF THE
UNDERGROUND RAILROAD

WRITTEN BY BARBARA GREENWOOD
ILLUSTRATED BY HEATHER COLLINS

KIDS CAN PRESS

For my children: Edward, Martha, Adrienne and Michael — great readers all.

BG

For my favorite designer, Blair.

HC

Canadian Cataloguing in Publication Data

Greenwood, Barbara, 1940-
 The Last Safe House : a story of the underground railroad

Includes index.
ISBN 1-55074-507-7 (bound)   ISBN 1-55074-509-3 (pbk.)

1. Underground railroad — Juvenile literature. 2. Fugitive slaves — United States — Juvenile literature. 3. Fugitive slaves — Canada — Juvenile literature. 4. Underground railroad — Juvenile fiction. 5. Fugitive slaves — United States — Juvenile fiction. 6. Fugitive slaves — Canada — Juvenile fiction. I. Collins, Heather. II. Title.

E450.G73 1998   j973.7'115   C98-930345-4

Text copyright ©1998 by Barbara Greenwood
Illustrations copyright © 1998 by Heather Collins

We acknowledge the support of the Canada Council for the Arts and the Ontario Arts Council for our publishing program.

Published in Canada by
Kids Can Press Ltd.
29 Birch Avenue
Toronto, ON M4V 1E2

Published in the U.S. by
Kids Can Press Ltd.
85 River Rock Drive, Suite 202
Buffalo, NY 14207

Edited by Valerie Wyatt
Designed by Blair Kerrigan/Glyphics
Music (pages 92-93) arranged by Matt Dewar

Printed and bound in Canada by Kromar Printing
CM 98 0 9 8 7 6 5 4 3 2 1
PA CM 98 0 9 8 7 6 5 4 3 2 1

Acknowledgments

This is a story of a family in St. Catharines, Canada West, in 1856, whose lives are changed when they are asked to help Eliza Jackson, a black girl escaping from slavery. Although the families are fictional, the background is fact, based on information from many reliable sources.

 I am indebted to Daniel G. Hill's authoritative history of the life of escaped slaves in Canada, *The Freedom Seekers: Blacks in Early Canada* (The Book Society of Canada/Stoddart, 1981), and to a number of museums that house artifacts and collections pertaining to black history. The North American Black Historical Museum and Cultural Centre in Amherstburg, Ontario was particularly useful. These, along with many other sources, helped me understand the realities of the Canadian portion of the Underground Railroad. Along with various social histories of the time, they also helped me envision Johanna's initial reaction to the arrival of Eliza Jackson and her subsequent growth in understanding.

 In creating the background for my fictional Jackson family, I drew on many first-person accounts of escapes. Particularly useful was Benjamin Drew's *The Narratives of Fugitive Slaves in Canada*, published in 1856. William Still also recorded the stories of escaped slaves who passed through his safe house in Philadelphia. Many of these appear in Charles L. Blockson's *The Underground Railroad* (Prentice-Hall, 1987). Blockson's *The Hippocrene Guide to the Underground Railroad* (Hippocrene, 1994) provided detailed information on various escape routes.

 A book of this nature needs a talented illustrator dedicated to historical accuracy. Many thanks to Heather Collins, not only for her painstaking attention to detail but also for the warmth and energy her art projects. And more thanks than I can express to two people who gave me constant encouragement and support through all the vicissitudes of such a large project: my husband and tireless researcher, Robert E. Greenwood, and my editor, Valerie Wyatt, who combines great creativity and sensitivity with her impressive editing skills.

CONTENTS

Introduction 4

Midnight Guest 6

Eliza's Story 24

Ben on the Run 44

Outsiders 62

Slave Catcher! 76

Friends 94

Six Months Later 105

Glossary 117

Bibliography 118

Index 119

INTRODUCTION

This is the story of two families who meet in June of 1856.

The Jacksons are fleeing a life of slavery in the southern United States. The Reids live in St. Catharines, Canada West (now Ontario), a community that received hundreds of escaped slaves and helped them find new homes in Canada.

It is also a story of the Underground Railroad, a network of people who passed fugitive slaves in secret, by night, north to freedom. The routes the fleeing slaves used were kept such well-guarded secrets that even today we know only a fragment of the whole story.

The Underground Railroad began in the early 1800s and lasted until 1865. This book tells the fictional story of one family of fugitives and the true stories of many real people who fled to freedom or worked on the Underground Railroad.

Although the Reids and the Jacksons are made-up families, they are typical of many Canadians and Americans who put into action their belief that all people should live in freedom.

Mrs. Leah Jackson   Eliza Jackson   Ben Jackson

Johanna Reid   Mr. Reid   Mrs. Reid   Tom Reid

MIDNIGHT GUEST

Johanna woke with a start. She listened for the sound that had pierced her sleep. The house was silent except for the wind rustling the elms outside her window. She drew a shaky breath. A nightmare, that's all it was, a nightmare.

"No! No! Don't . . . Help!"

Johanna sat bolt upright. She *hadn't* imagined it. "Mother," she tried to call, but her voice was no more than a croak.

In the bedroom across the hall, a match flared and a candle sprang to light. "Mother!" Johanna tried again, but the light whisked past, throwing her mother's shadow briefly on the wall. The room went dark again and Johanna heard a new sound. Was it sobbing?

And then her father was striding down the hall. His presence made her brave. She slid out of bed and hurried after him. Light from the small candle outlined her father and brother, Tom, hovering at the sewing-room door. She crept nearer, and as she slipped between them, her father held out an arm and drew her close.

"Momma . . . Where's my momma?" The wail broke on a shuddery sob.

Johanna could see her mother bending over the cot that stood against one wall of the room. "What's going on?" she whispered.

Tom started to answer. "She's . . ."

"Go back to bed," her father interrupted quietly. "Your mother will deal with this."

Johanna craned around him. "But who's in there?" There was no answer, only her father's strong hand on the small of her back urging her along the hall. Tom had already disappeared into his room. Did he know what this was all about?

"Time enough in the morning for explanations." Her father's tone was sharper this time. "Go back to sleep."

Sleep? How can I possibly sleep? Johanna crawled into bed, shivering even though the June night was warm. There's nothing to be afraid of. Calm yourself. But when she closed her eyes questions crowded into her mind.

Why the secrecy? They often had guests, but she was always told about them, usually had to make up the bed and tidy the room. Mind you, now that she thought back, something odd *had* been going on. Quizzical looks, lifted eyebrows, half-finished sentences when she came across her parents talking together. And then, this afternoon, a wagon rattling to a brief stop beside her as she walked home from the store. The driver had leaned over. "Message for your pa," he'd said quietly. "Parcel arrives on the evening train." She'd assumed he meant a package from Toronto. Could the message have had another meaning? Tomorrow, she thought, first thing tomorrow I'll find out what's going on.

Johanna woke to kitchen sounds, her head aching from the broken sleep. With bright sunlight chasing away the night fears, she felt vaguely resentful. Tom knows, she decided, so why not me? I can keep a secret.

Dressed and with her bed made, Johanna stepped into the hall and glanced toward the sewing room. The door was ajar. All was silent. She tiptoed along the hall and sidled through the doorway. A small shape, completely covered by the quilt, was curled in the middle of the small bed. As Johanna turned to leave, she heard a sigh. The sleeping guest rolled over and the edge of the quilt flipped down. Johanna gasped. The face, still stained with tears, was black.

Who is she? A girl about my age, but . . . Johanna thought about her father's customers. Some, certainly, were black — escaped slaves who had fled to St. Catharines. Could this girl be one of them? But why was she in their house?

The girl's eyes opened, then widened in alarm. She scrambled to the head of the bed, pressing herself against the wall. In her arms she clutched a doll. My china doll! Johanna had to stop herself from snatching it away. As though reading her mind, the girl dropped the doll on the quilt and pressed herself harder against the wall.

Footsteps clattered up the stairs. Johanna turned to the door but her mother brushed past her. "It's all right, Eliza." Mrs. Reid's voice was soft and soothing, the voice she used to calm fretful babies. "There's nothing to be frightened of. It's just Johanna."

The girl swallowed and nodded as Mrs. Reid patted her hand. Then Mrs. Reid turned toward Johanna. "Eliza's had a bad scare," she said. "Come downstairs and I'll explain while we make breakfast." She stroked Eliza's head. "Now, don't you worry. Everything's all right. You rest and I'll bring you something to eat."

"She's a slave, isn't she?" Johanna asked abruptly when they were in the kitchen.

"Escaped slave," her mother corrected. "And not out of danger yet."

"But she's in Canada. They're free here. Orrin Brown told me he kissed the ground when he stepped off the ferry because he'd never be a slave again."

"Things have changed since Orrin arrived. Slave catchers are coming right across the border now, bold as brass. Why, just a few weeks back, you remember, they nabbed a fugitive down in Windsor. Dragged him onto the ferry in broad daylight. How people could just stand and watch . . . " As she spoke, Mrs. Reid stoked up the stove and set out a large frying pan. "Help me with breakfast, Johanna. Your father will be back any minute now."

By the time Johanna had fried ham slices, ladled out porridge and poured boiling water over tea leaves in the large brown pot, she had heard as much as Mrs. Reid knew of their guest's story — how Eliza escaped from a plantation with her mother and brother, how they traveled from one safe house to another, always heading north. Then their luck turned bad. One night tracking dogs picked up their trail and they had to separate. When they reached the next safe house, there was no sign of her brother, Ben. So Eliza and her mother had to go on without him. But that wasn't the worst of it. A few days later the slave catchers found them, caught Mrs. Jackson and nearly got Eliza, too.

"No wonder she's had nightmares, poor child," Mrs. Reid said.

"But how did she get *here*?"

"Abram Fuller brought her. Fetched her from the American side in a rowboat, after dark last night. He's brought so many slaves across the river lately that his house is being watched. So he brought her here."

Johanna turned this information over in her mind as she set the table. All very well for Mr. Fuller, she thought, but there'd been all sorts of whispering about town. Not everyone welcomed the escaped slaves flooding across the river. What if the girls at school found out? "Is she staying with us?"

"For a while. We'll keep her hidden until Mr. Fuller sends word about her family. Then we'll have to get her to a safer place."

Johanna turned away to hide the sudden relief she felt. Yes, let's keep her a secret. She can stay for a few nights — as long as no one finds out.

After breakfast, Mrs. Reid said, "Have a look through those dresses in the blanket box, Johanna. Eliza's clothes are in tatters after all she's been through."

Sorting through the outgrown dresses, Johanna came across her favorite blue gingham. Her mother had used the leftovers from it to dress Clara, her china doll. The thought of Clara in the stranger's arms irritated her all over again, and now her mother wanted her to be nice to Eliza. She needs someone to talk to, her mother had said. About what? Johanna wondered, folding the blue gingham away carefully. What could we possibly have to talk about? She pulled out an old brown linsey-woolsey and held it up. This will do, she thought.

Eliza was sitting on a chair in the sewing room, her hands folded tightly in her lap, when Johanna came in with the dress. Clara sat primly on the table, her skirts and petticoats spread in a neat circle.

Johanna cast about for something to say. "Mother doesn't think you'll have to stay cooped up in this tiny room for long."

Eliza darted a glance at the dress Johanna had laid on the bed, then looked down at her tightly folded hands. "Place Mist' Fuller fetched me from was lots smaller'n this." Her voice was no more than a whisper.

"Whatever do you mean?"

Eliza sighed, then put out a hand to stroke the dress. "We was headed for our last stop on the Underground Railroad." Her voice was so low, Johanna had to strain to hear. "Freedom's just a step away, they said. Look for the lantern in the upstairs window and we'd be safe." She paused and glanced up at Johanna. Then she looked down at her hands again.

"So we walked all night. I was near to droppin' by the time we saw the light. Just afore dawn it was, but the missus, she took us into the kitchen, nice as anything. 'Just set there a minute,' she says. 'I'll stir up this

fire and make you some breakfast.' Pan fries, it was. My mouth could just about taste 'em." A smile flickered across Eliza's face, then died. "Heard a great fuss out in the yard. Shoutin' and I don't know what. The missus, she grabs me and stuffs me into a hidey-hole in the wall. 'Stay quiet,' she says, and slides a little door across."

Johanna heard a catch in Eliza's voice. The girl folded her thin arms around her body and started to rock back and forth. She's going to cry again, Johanna thought. As she turned to shout for her mother, she glimpsed the doll. Catching it up from the table, she held it out. Eliza reached for the doll and buried her face in its silky brown hair. After a moment the whispery voice continued.

"Just like being in a coffin, it was. No room to stretch or turn. But I could hear, clear as day. Shoutin' and boots stompin' down the stairs and then — shriekin' an' cryin'. And me clawin' at the door because that was my momma. But try as I might, I couldn't shift that door. Nothin' I could do. Just laid my face on that dusty floor an' cried and cried."

Eliza's voice trailed off. She dashed tears from her cheeks. "Musta fell asleep. Next thing I know, there's hands pullin' at me and me fightin' them. Then I see it's the missus. She sets me on my feet. Nearly fell over, I was so stiff. And then she tells me. Slave catcher has my momma."

Eliza stopped again and squeezed her eyes shut to hold back the tears. She drew a ragged breath, then she set her jaw and said through clenched teeth, "But she promised they'd find her. And Mist' Fuller, he promised they'd find her an' . . . an' I know my momma will fight them." Then the fierceness went out of her voice. Her shoulders sagged. "But I don't know." She nestled one cheek into the doll's hair. "Bad things happen."

All the rest of the day, Johanna thought about Eliza's story. As she ironed and folded, peeled and chopped, washed and dried, pictures flashed through her mind — the tiny, dark hiding place in the wall, the booted men on the stairs, the screaming woman. Was the same slave catcher still after Eliza?

"What I don't understand," Johanna said late that afternoon as she sat helping her mother peel potatoes, "is why a slave catcher would bother with Eliza. She's just a girl, not even as old as me."

Mrs. Reid pursed her lips. "Everything to do with slavery is hard to understand." She put down her knife and sighed. "According to Abram Fuller, Eliza and her mother are good household servants. That makes them valuable."

"Even so, to come all the way to Canada . . ."

"Mr. Fuller says their owner has offered a very large reward. Enough to make it worthwhile for a slave catcher to cross the border. It's happened before, Johanna. People who thought they were safe . . . No one must know she's here. You understand, don't you?"

Johanna nodded. But what if he *does* show up here? The thought made her hand tremble so that the paring knife slipped and drew a bead of blood. What would we do? What *could* we do?

THE UNDERGROUND RAILROAD

The Reids' house in St. Catharines, Canada West (now Ontario), was the end of a long, dangerous and frightening journey for Eliza. When she and her family ran away from a small plantation in Virginia, they knew only that freedom lay far to the north. They had also heard the rumor, whispered at night in the slave quarters, that somewhere there was a road, an underground railroad, that would carry them to freedom.

There was not, of course, an actual road running underground. But there was a network of farmers and townsfolk who worked in secret to pass the runaways from one safe house to another. They were angry about the treatment of the slaves, who were often whipped the moment they were caught. So they began watching out for fugitives and hiding them in their homes and barns until the pursuers gave up and left. Then they gave the runaways food for their journey and information to help them find their way north.

How did this pathway to freedom get such a strange name? In 1831, a plantation owner chasing a fugitive slave named Tice Davids reported that he'd almost caught the runaway, practically had him in his hands, when he seemed to disappear into thin air. No matter how hard he searched, the owner never set eyes on Davids again. "It was almost," the baffled plantation owner said, "as though he'd disappeared onto an underground road." Later the name was changed to Underground Railroad because the fugitives seemed to move as fast as the new steam trains that crisscrossed the country.

Before 1850, slaves were free once they reached a northern state that had outlawed slavery. But the Fugitive Slave law of 1850 forced all Americans, even those in free states, to help slave owners capture escaped slaves. As a result, fugitives had to travel farther north to Canada to find freedom. Even then they needed help to stay out of the clutches of slave catchers.

Some "stations" had hidden rooms and tunnels leading to secret forest paths.

KEEPING THE SECRET

"Parcel arrives on the evening train." This sounds like a straightforward message, but to a person who recognized the code, it carried a hidden meaning. When Mrs. Reid heard it, she knew a fugitive would arrive that evening.

Code words were essential to keep the activities of the Underground Railroad secret. The runaways were called "parcels" or "freight." The person showing them the way was a "conductor." The safe houses were "stations" and the people running them "station agents." Using these code words, a message was sent to alert the next station to prepare for the arrival of a fugitive. If the message fell into the wrong hands, it would be taken for news about a shipment arriving by train.

Codes were used by slaves long before they made contact with the Underground Railroad. Many used music to send messages from plantation to plantation. Someone singing about "crossing the river" was passing on information about how to escape by crossing the Ohio River into a free state. "Canaan" and the "Promised Land" were often used as code words for Canada. A slave singing "Steal away, steal away, steal away to Jesus" was alerting other slaves that an escape attempt was coming up. When the punishment for doing or saying anything that angered the owners was a flogging, slaves needed secret ways to communicate just to survive.

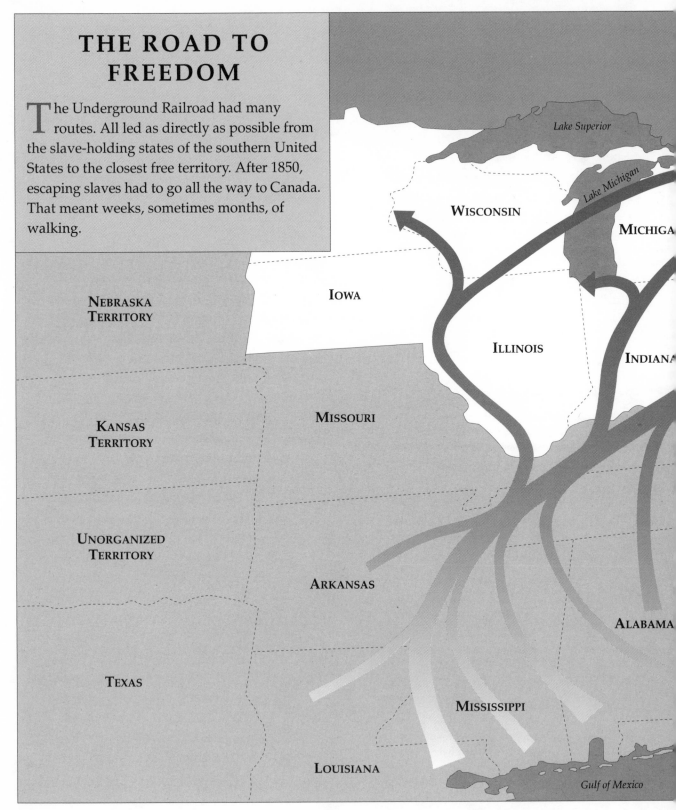

THE ROAD TO FREEDOM

The Underground Railroad had many routes. All led as directly as possible from the slave-holding states of the southern United States to the closest free territory. After 1850, escaping slaves had to go all the way to Canada. That meant weeks, sometimes months, of walking.

Lake Superior

Lake Michigan

WISCONSIN

MICHIGAN

IOWA

NEBRASKA TERRITORY

ILLINOIS

INDIANA

KANSAS TERRITORY

MISSOURI

UNORGANIZED TERRITORY

ARKANSAS

ALABAMA

TEXAS

MISSISSIPPI

LOUISIANA

Gulf of Mexico

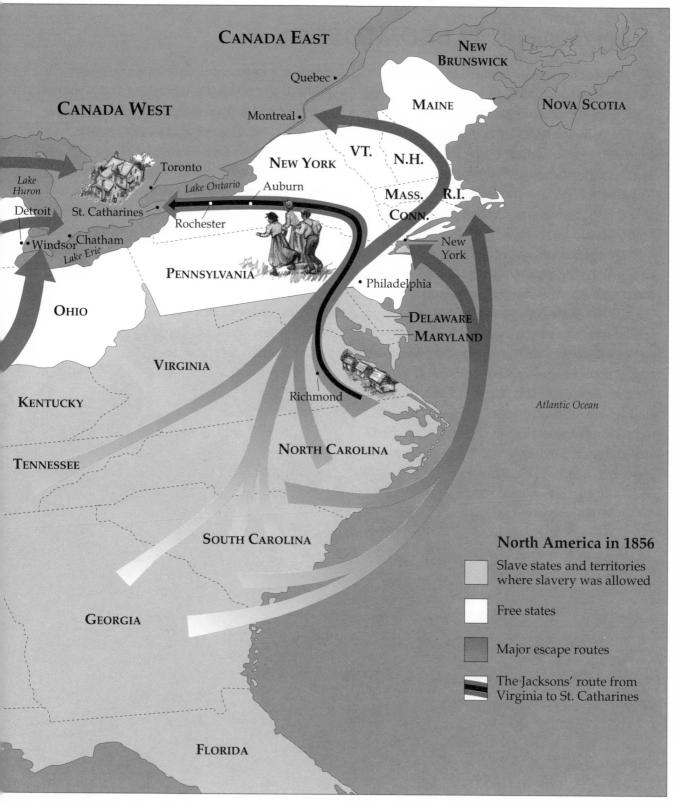

CANADA EAST

CANADA WEST

Quebec •

NEW
BRUNSWICK

NOVA SCOTIA

MAINE

Montreal •

Lake
Huron

Toronto

Lake Ontario

VT.

NEW YORK

N.H.

Detroit •

St. Catharines

Auburn

MASS.

R.I.

• Windsor • Chatham
Lake Erie

Rochester

CONN.

New
York

PENNSYLVANIA

• Philadelphia

OHIO

DELAWARE
MARYLAND

KENTUCKY

VIRGINIA

Atlantic Ocean

• Richmond

TENNESSEE

NORTH CAROLINA

SOUTH CAROLINA

North America in 1856

Slave states and territories
where slavery was allowed

GEORGIA

Free states

Major escape routes

FLORIDA

The Jacksons' route from
Virginia to St. Catharines

SOLD INTO SLAVERY

Eliza was born a slave, just as her mother and grandmother had been. But Eliza's great-grandmother was born free, on the west coast of Africa. She grew up in a village where she was loved and happy. One day, while she was walking through the jungle with a group of other young people, men jumped across the trail in front of them. The group turned to flee, only to find more men behind them. Some of the strongest young men escaped, but Eliza's great-grandmother and six of her friends were knocked to the ground. Chained to one another, they were forced to walk out of the jungle, away from their village, toward the sea and waiting ships.

The kidnapped young people were herded onto a ship and forced down into the hold with many other prisoners. There, they were packed in like cargo and chained together so closely they could barely move. Fed poorly and in despair because they had been stolen from their homes, many of these young men and women did not survive the six-week voyage across the Atlantic Ocean.

For those who did survive, worse was to come in the new land. They were sold to plantation owners in the southern United States who used whips to force them to work from sunup to sundown. Under the blistering sun, they planted, hoed and harvested sugar cane, tobacco, rice and cotton. Some rebelled and ran off into the swamps and forests, but often starvation drove them back to the plantation. The brutal floggings they received as punishment were used to warn others against running away. Most slaves simply worked until they died under the lash or from disease or exhaustion.

In the 250 years that slavery lasted in the United States, millions of people were sold into bondage so that plantation owners could grow rich selling the sugar, tobacco, rice and cotton grown by their captive laborers.

The misery, fear and longing for home the slaves felt came out in the songs they sang and the stories they told. Later generations of slaves often used stories from the Bible to express their longing for freedom. In one famous song they sang:

Go down, Moses, way down in Egypt land
Tell old Pharaoh to "let my people go."

ELIZA'S STORY

"How did you know where to go?" Johanna asked, as the two girls rolled out cookie dough on the kitchen table.

"Followed the North Star. That's all we knew. Follow the North Star to Canada, the Promised Land."

"The Promised Land? You mean like in the Bible?"

"The very one!" Eliza's face lit up. "A land flowin' with milk and honey, my momma says."

Johanna gave the dough a last roll. Milk and honey! She thought about her arms aching after milking their Daisy and the stings she'd got while gathering honey. Milk and honey don't flow around here without a lot of hard work, she thought.

Not that Eliza shirked hard work. For three days she'd been hidden upstairs while the Reids went about their business, alert for news of strangers. "Can't just sit idle," she'd said, stitching away at the brown linsey-woolsey dress. Rolled carefully on the table beside her was the thread she'd unpicked. "Dress is enough," she'd said. "No need to trouble you for thread."

And this morning, the first day she'd been allowed downstairs, Eliza had immediately pitched in to help with the bread making, then offered to make gingerbread cookies "just like my momma's."

Now, with the dough rolled thin on the table, the girls were stamping out cookies. Johanna slid the last of the circles off the spatula onto the cookie tray. "All done," she sighed, wiping floury hands down her apron.

Eliza was hunched over a triangle of dough, tracing something with the point of a knife. Johanna leaned across to have a look, and Eliza glanced up shyly.

"That's me," she said, flicking the extra dough away from a striding figure. "Runnin' away from the fox. You know that story? I ran away from the little old woman and the little old man — " Johanna chimed in, "And I can run away from you, I can." Eliza clapped her hands and laughed. That's the first time she's laughed since she got here, Johanna realized. Must be the message from Mr. Fuller. "May have located lost parcel," it had read. "Will forward when verified."

"Reckon that story saved my life," Eliza said as she opened the oven door for Johanna.

"How was that?" Day by day they'd heard more of Eliza's story. Just snippets at first, told in a shy whisper, but they'd soon realized that Eliza was a born storyteller. Even Tom was spellbound. Last evening Johanna had caught him sitting on the stairs outside the sewing room, listening to Eliza spin stories as she stitched.

"Goodness, girls, aren't you done yet?" Mrs. Reid bustled in from the parlor where she'd been filling the oil lamps. "We'll have to get started at the noon meal soon."

Eliza muttered, "Sorry, missus," but Johanna just raised an eyebrow at her mother's retreating back. It wouldn't take a minute to wash up, for goodness' sake.

Eliza started scrubbing down the table, using a knife to scrape the leftover flour and bits of dough into the mixing bowl.

"Oh, that can wait," Johanna said, sitting down. "The washing-up water hasn't even boiled yet. First I want to know how that story saved your life." She waved at a chair and Eliza flopped down, arms leaning on the kitchen table. Her eyes glazed with a faraway look.

"It was right after Ben went missin'," she started, and for a second her eyes clouded. "Man helpin' us says we gotta move along fast. So we come into a little town flat out on the bottom of a wagon, under a load of hay. Nothing so prickly as hay when you have to keep still. And the bouncin'! Near shook us to pieces. Drove right into the barn so's no one would see us. We'd just crawled out of that scratchy old hay pile when the missus come runnin'.

"'Get them out of here,' she says, all panicky. 'Two men just rode into town with a marshal.' She was real scared. Big trouble for them if they was caught helping us. The man tells us to get back in the wagon and he'll take us to the next safe house. But my momma, she's looking out the barn door and she says, 'Scuse me, missus. Notice you got laundry all bundled up. How's if we carry it on down the street like we's taking it for washin'?' The man, he thinks that's a mighty fine idea. 'Watch for a house with two sycamores out front,' he says."

Just then the kettle started to burble.

"Don't stop! Don't stop!" Johanna jumped up to pour hot water over the dishes in the washing-up bowl. But nothing could stop Eliza now. On she went as they washed and dried and put away.

"My heart was near poundin' out of my chest. Walk down the middle of the street, right under the noses of those slave catchers? Laws! But my momma says, 'Liza, you remember that gingerbread boy? Well, *we* run away from the little old man and the little old woman. No reason on God's green earth why we can't run away from the fox.'"

Eliza's eyes danced. "And she was right. We marched down that street with laundry on our heads like we belonged. My heart near jumped into my mouth when those men come clip-cloppin' up the street. Momma, she says, 'Keep your eyes down and your back straight.' Then she sails right on past them, with me comin' along behind. In no time, we were at the safe house, creepin' like moles through a tunnel into the woods. And my momma squeezin' my hand and whisperin', 'Fooled you, Mr. Fox.'"

And Eliza was up, whirling about the room. "Fooled you, Mr. Fox. Fooled you!"

"Look out!" Johanna cried, just too late. The mixing bowl Eliza had been clutching sailed out of her arms and smashed against the stove.

Mrs. Reid whisked back into the kitchen. "Really, girls," she said crossly.

Eliza's face went blank. Then suddenly she was shrinking into the corner, covering her head with her arms. "Sorry, missus, sorry . . . didn't mean . . . sorry." With each "sorry" she cowered farther into the corner.

Mrs. Reid's frown softened. "My dear, it's all right," she said quietly. "It's just a bowl."

Eliza nodded and crept out of the corner. She scooped the pieces into her apron and backed away, flinching as Mrs. Reid reached to take them from her.

Why, she's terrified, Johanna thought, terrified of my mother, who wouldn't harm a soul.

Even when her gingerbread girl came out of the oven, Eliza was quiet. After she'd helped peel potatoes she said in a subdued voice, "Better go back upstairs."

Johanna and her mother worked on in silence. Finally Johanna burst out, "Why all that over a broken bowl?"

Mrs. Reid gave the gravy a few more stirs, then she sighed. "You know what your father says — you can always tell if a dog's been mistreated. I imagine it's the same with a person."

"But a broken bowl? You wouldn't . . . "

"No, but where Eliza's been, from the stories I've heard . . ."

"You mean she's been beaten for breaking something?"

"Or for a lot less, I'll wager. You know what Orrin Brown told us — a lot of the owners treat their slaves like animals. Beat them for any little thing. Eliza doesn't understand that things are different here." Then, in her usual brisk tone, "Now go and bring her down for dinner. It's just ready to go on the table."

Johanna turned slowly toward the stairs. What could she possibly say to reassure Eliza? Then she saw, cooling on the window ledge, Eliza's gingerbread girl. Carefully she picked it up and started upstairs.

Eliza was rocking as she sat on the bed, the china doll in her arms. She seemed to be murmuring into its ear. When she saw Johanna she sat up straight and thrust the doll away.

"It's all right," Johanna said. "You can play . . . you can hold her."

"I had a doll. My momma made it for me." Eliza smoothed the china doll's blue gingham skirt lovingly. "She was carryin' it for me in her apron pocket when those men snatched her."

Johanna struggled for words to comfort Eliza. Should she remind her about Mr. Fuller's note? But what if he hadn't found Ben? Then she remembered the gingerbread girl. "Look!" She held it out to Eliza. "It's you — running free."

Eliza looked at the little figure for a long minute. "No." She shook her head. "Not free. Just runnin'. Til they find my momma and Ben — just runnin'."

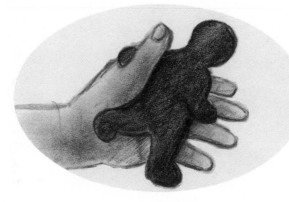

A COTTON PLANTATION

The Jacksons' run for freedom started on a plantation in Virginia. A plantation is a large farm on which one main crop is grown. In some areas of the southern States the crop was tobacco. Sugar or rice was grown in hot, moist areas. But the most important crop was cotton.

Plantations were far from towns, so each one had to produce all the food, clothing and goods that the owner and the slaves needed.

Food for the owner's family is grown in the kitchen garden.

Garden produce is stored behind a locked door. The owner's wife carries the keys.

Hams and strings of sausages hang in the locked smokehouse.

In the well house, water running over stone floors keeps milk and butter cool.

A slave trained as a cooper makes all the barrels, buckets, tubs and churns.

The stables house the master's riding horses and the mules, which are used for the hardest labor.

A slave trained as a blacksmith works at the forge. He shoes the horses and makes and repairs tools and household items.

The owner, or master, and his family live in the Big House.

In the laundry, slaves wash and iron clothes for the owner's family.

In several small buildings, slaves make soap and candles or weave, dye and sew cloth.

The kitchen, with its large fireplace, is in a separate building, to keep the Big House cool.

Rows of cabins make up the slave quarters. Often a family of six or eight lives in one cabin.

WORKING IN THE BIG HOUSE

When Eliza was born, her mother prayed that her daughter would be trained to work in the Big House, where the master and his family lived. Household work was hard but it was not as backbreaking as working in the fields from sunup to sundown. So Leah Jackson was delighted when her mistress decided that Eliza, at six years old, would begin to learn how to cook, sew and help with the laundry.

COOKING

In the kitchen building, the mistress supervised one or two slaves in the work of preserving the garden produce and cooking the meals for the family. There was no stove, only a large fireplace where geese, chickens, pork and even opossum were cooked. Sweet potatoes and collard greens boiled with peas were favorite vegetables. Eliza helped by shelling peas and turning geese roasting on the spit.

Every morning Leah Jackson got up early to make spoon bread or corn bread for the master's breakfast. Once a week she baked yeast bread. Then, while the oven was still hot, she put in cakes, pies and cookies. As Eliza pitted cherries or cut out molasses cookies with a cup, she watched her mother and learned how to cook and bake for the family in the Big House.

SEWING

Every year the mistress bought bolts of cotton cloth and linsey-woolsey, a combination of wool and linen or cotton, to make summer and winter clothes for the slaves. Eliza learned to sew by helping her mother and the other slave women make dozens of simple shirts, pants and skirts. She also helped piece together the scraps for quilts.

All the sewing was done by hand, even after sewing machines became available in 1845. In the south there were always enough hands to do the work the old-fashioned way. Because Leah was a fine seamstress, she often made frilled petticoats and drawers for the master's children. Once she was allowed to use leftover scraps of blue calico to dress a doll for Eliza.

LAUNDRY

On washing day, Leah started by boiling all the white things in a big copper boiler. She put the dyed clothes in a tub of warm water so they wouldn't fade. Then she scrubbed soiled spots on a wooden washboard. With a large pronged stick she lifted the soapy clothes into tubs of cool rinse water. She used a wooden wringer to squeeze water out of the heavy sheets. Small things were wrung out by hand.

Eliza helped by spreading handkerchiefs and collars on the grass to dry and bleach in the sun. She stretched damp stockings over foot-shaped boards to keep them from shrinking. By the time the laundry was hung out to dry everyone was exhausted. But the work was far from over. It took most of the next day to do the ironing.

Making Gingerbread Cookies

One of the specialties Leah made for the master's children was gingerbread. At Christmas she cut out little gingerbread people for the children to string with dried cranberries.

You can make gingerbread cookies or a running gingerbread figure like the one Eliza cut out.

You'll need:

- 75 mL (1/3 c.) butter
- 75 mL (1/3 c.) brown sugar
- 1 egg, well beaten
- 15 mL (1 tbsp.) baking powder
- pinch of salt
- 5 mL (1 tsp.) ground ginger
- pinch of ground allspice or cloves
- 10 mL (2 tsp.) ground cinnamon
- 750 mL (3 c.) flour
- 150 mL (2/3 c.) molasses
- currants or raisins for decoration

1. Ask an adult to turn the oven to 200 °C (400 °F).

2. In a large bowl, mix together the butter and brown sugar until creamy. Stir in the beaten egg.

3. Put baking powder, salt, all the spices and flour into a sifter and sift them into another large bowl.

4. To the first mixture add a spoonful of the dry ingredients and mix well. Then add a spoonful of molasses and mix well. Continue until all the dry ingredients and molasses are used up. The dough will be stiff.

5. Turn the dough onto a square of wax paper. Roll it up and refrigerate for two hours.

6. Sprinkle some flour onto the counter and roll out the dough to a thickness of 0.5 cm (1/4 in.).

7. Cut out gingerbread figures or other shapes. Make faces and buttons from currants or raisins. Use a spatula to transfer the cookies to a baking tray that has been greased with butter.

8. Ask an adult to put the tray into the oven. Bake for ten minutes.

9. Use a spatula to transfer the cookies to a rack. Let them cool.

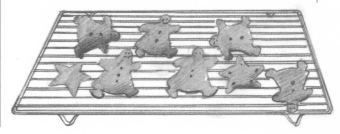

DECIDING TO RUN

"That girl's coming up 11. Bright, well trained and biddable. And the boy's good and strong. They'd fetch a fine price at auction. And we could sure do with the money."

Those words struck terror into Leah Jackson's heart. She'd worked hard for her owners and made her children behave well in the hope that this would be their home forever. But now the master was talking about putting Eliza and Ben on the auction block.

Selling slaves was not unusual. Owners had complete control over their slaves' lives. They decided where slaves lived, what they worked at, and how many hours a day they worked. They also had the right to sell their slaves, even if it meant breaking up families.

Slaves were sold at auction in the town marketplace. Here the slaves stood up on platforms, called auction blocks, so that customers could look them over and bid for them.

Leah herself had gone to the auction block once. Back when she was a young mother she had worked on a large plantation as a laundress and cook. Her husband, Sam, was the plantation blacksmith. They were useful and well-thought-of by the master's family. Then one day Sam learned that his brother and three other slaves were to be sold to pay the master's gambling debts. He knew what that meant. The best way to make money was to sell slaves "down the river," to a cotton plantation on the southern Mississippi River. There, brutal overseers worked the field hands almost to death. Sam's strong, young brother would fetch more than $1000 from a cotton grower.

After midnight, reckless with grief and rage, Sam slipped out to the shed where his brother and the others were manacled to a post. Using his black-smith's tools he snapped their chains, then he watched them run off into the night. Somehow the master found out. As punishment, Sam himself was sold south. Leah, with her baby and toddler, was also sent to the auction block. The master didn't want any rebellious slaves on his plantation.

Leah never forgot the humiliation of standing up on the auction block while buyers looked her up and down as though she were a prize mare. She was determined that her children would never suffer that fate, even if it meant running away.

Like many other slaves who had decided to run, Leah sang in her heart what she didn't dare breathe out loud until she reached freedom:

> *No more auction block for me,*
> *No more, no more.*
> *No more auction block for me.*
> *Many thousand gone.*

Follow the North Star

When Eliza and her family started out for Canada, they had no maps, only a saying to guide them: "Follow the North Star."

Sailors and explorers have always used the stars to help them find their way. To sight the stars, they had instruments called astrolabes. Fugitive slaves had no such instruments. Instead, they used a constellation called the Big Dipper to help them find the North Star.

You too can find the North Star.

Look for the Big Dipper. Find the two stars that form the side of the dipper farthest from the handle. Imagine a line joining these stars and continuing out into the sky. Look for a bright star all by itself along this line. This is Polaris, or the North Star. When you are facing Polaris you are facing north.

Polaris
(The North
Star)

The Big
Dipper

On clear nights, the Jacksons set their course by the North Star. One night when clouds blocked their view, Ben remembered a hint he'd been given at the start of their journey: moss is always thickest on the north side of a tree. Look for moss growing up the trunks of trees. See if you can find north this way.

SLAVERY IN CANADA

Slaves who had heard that freedom lay to the north thought of Canada as the Promised Land. But Canada had not always been a land of freedom.

Early settlers needed laborers to help clear the land. Some bought slaves from the American colonies to the south. Others enslaved Native people. More slaves arrived when the American Revolution broke out in 1775. Many fleeing American colonists brought their black slaves to Nova Scotia and Quebec.

John Graves Simcoe, Lieutenant Governor of Upper Canada (now Ontario), tried to abolish slavery in 1793, but too many influential families were slaveholders. He *did* pass a law saying that no more slaves could be brought into Upper Canada and that children born to slaves already in the colony would automatically become free at age 25. The law also made owners accountable if they mistreated their slaves. By 1834, when the British government abolished slavery in all its colonies, Canada was already slave free.

After the United States passed the Fugitive Slave law in 1850, forcing all Americans to return runaways to their owners, Canada became the slaves' only safe haven. Many Canadians were strongly anti-slavery. In 1851 the Anti-Slavery Society of Canada was formed in Toronto to help abolish slavery and house and clothe black fugitives. Other cities and towns had similar organizations.

By 1863, when the Emancipation Proclamation finally freed all slaves in the United States, as many as 60 000 fugitive slaves had found freedom, safety and a new life in Canada.

THE ABOLITIONISTS

People who fought to have slavery made illegal called themselves abolitionists because they wanted to abolish, or completely do away with, a practice they felt was wrong.

Among the earliest abolitionists was the Society of Friends, a religious group often called Quakers. They believed that all people were equal in the sight of God. The Quakers not only refused to own slaves, they believed it was their duty to help slaves escape to freedom. Often they were fined or jailed for their actions.

Abolitionists tried many different ways to change public opinion about slavery. Harriet Beecher Stowe used the power of a story to make people think. In her novel, *Uncle Tom's Cabin*, she told the story of a kindly old slave beaten by a cruel master named Simon Legree. It convinced many people in the northern states that slavery had to be abolished. When war was declared between the northern and southern states, the story of Uncle Tom was one of the reasons northerners were so willing to fight.

LEVI COFFIN

The most famous Quaker abolitionist was Levi Coffin. He and his wife, Catherine, lived in Newport (now Fountain City), Indiana, on a route of the Underground Railroad. By building hidden rooms and cellars in their home, they were able to hide many runaways. Later they continued their work in Cincinnati. For over 35 years they helped more than 2000 slaves on their way to freedom.

Although he and his wife gave much practical help to runaways, Levi Coffin is best known for influencing others to get involved. He was a successful storekeeper and business people trusted him. When he needed money to help the conductors and station agents on the Underground Railroad buy food and clothing, he was able to raise it quickly from these contacts. He traveled up and down the Underground Railroad encouraging workers and seeing for himself that runaways were being treated well. He even visited Canada to see how runaways were settling into their new communities. Coffin's work for fugitive slaves earned him the honorary title of president of the Underground Railroad.

"Sixth night out there's a full moon. Near bright as day. Shoulda stayed put, but we kept goin' anyways. That's when they spotted us. A patrol with four dogs, huntin' hounds. 'Only chance,' Momma says, 'split up.' Closest cover's a big forest. I was lost in no time. Then come the swamp."

And suddenly he was back in that moment, with the muffled yelping of the hounds sounding behind him and a narrow trail twisting away into darkness before him. Had the dogs picked up his scent? As he pounded barefoot along the unfamiliar path he prayed for a creek he could run through to break his trail. Or should he climb a tree? Would that confuse the dogs? Or would he just be stuck up there waiting for them? Desperately he ran on, every bump and root on the path pummeling his feet until they went numb.

Something clutched at his ankle and he pitched headlong onto the hard-packed mud of the trail. Snake! He drew a sharp breath. No. Only a trailing vine tripping him up. He let out his breath slowly. Then he heard the dogs again, muffled but still following. Get up! Get up!

He put his palms flat on the ground and pushed. With a sickening squelch his right hand disappeared into slippery mud. His arm was buried past the elbow before he managed to wiggle backward, keeping his weight spread over the firm path behind. Slowly he pulled free of the mud's gluey grasp. One more step and he would have plunged right into those sucking sands and been swallowed alive. As his pounding heart slowed, he heard again, faint but following, the baying of hounds.

Despair washed over him. How could he find a way out? Crouching on the pathway staring into the dark, he imagined the tree limbs twisting and twining into an impenetrable wall ahead of him. But the urgency that had driven him this far kept prodding him. There must be a way. There must!

set out in a wagon hung about with lanterns and dippers an' I don't know what all. Under the floorboards there's a hidden cupboard. I crawl in there and off we go. Peddlin' to farmers all up and down the country."

"You could have suffocated!" Johanna exclaimed.

"Downright strangulated most of the time," Ben agreed. "And all that janglin' from the tinware! Near drove me silly. Just when it was comin' on for dark, my little cupboard door opens and Henry, he tells me it's the end of the line. Pretty soon I'm down a cellar ready to move on again."

"So," Mrs. Reid said with a satisfied sigh, "you *did* meet up with good people."

Ben thought about that for a moment and then nodded. In the end, he'd met only with kindness, despite Reuben's parting words. "Be vigilant, brother," Reuben had said, and his usual gentle smile was gone. "Your adversary, the devil, as a roaring lion walketh about, seeking whom he may devour."

And he *had* been vigilant, ready to run at the first sign of trouble. Every time he'd knocked on a door late at night and whispered the password, "A friend of a friend," his stomach had knotted in fear. Could there be others as willing as Reuben and Henry to risk their own safety? But each time the miracle had happened. An opened door, a whispered "Welcome, friend," and he was safe for one more day.

"How long did it take you?" Tom asked.

Ben thought for a moment. "Lost track," he said finally. "Full moon six nights after we run. Another some nights ago."

"Say a month and a bit," Tom decided. "A month of walking." He sounded impressed.

Ben looked at Eliza. She was the only one who really knew what that meant. Not just walking all night, but lying still as death under a load of manure as searchers challenged the driver, or squeezing through a narrow dirt tunnel from a safe house out to the surrounding woods. It wasn't the running. It was the fear.

"And now you're here," Eliza said softly. "Safe at last in our Promised Land."

That brought back another memory — his old master, laughing. "Canada? The Promised Land?" They'd been standing by the plantation gate looking down the road to where a black man in chains shuffled beside a horse and rider. It was Joe from the next place over. There'd been rumors he'd run away.

"You see that, boy?" Massa had said. "That's what thinking about Canada gets you. Didn't even make it through the swamp, that one. And what'll running get you anyway? Canada? It's so cold your toes'll drop right off. You know that ice I got packed in the icehouse? That's Canada — like livin' in that icehouse."

As cold as the icehouse? Ben looked around at the ring of welcoming smiles. No. Old Massa had been clean wrong about a lot of things. And, for sure, this was one. Whatever Canada was, it wasn't cold.

LIFE ON A PLANTATION

As Ben sat and ate with Henry and Reuben that night, they exchanged stories. Reuben told how he had started out life on a southern Mississippi River plantation. From the time he was five until he escaped at fifteen, he had worked in the fields, tending the cotton crop.

Large cotton plantations needed huge gangs of up to 200 workers. An overseer hired by the owner ran the plantation. He handed out each slave's daily task and saw that it was done properly.

For Reuben and the other slaves, life on the plantations of the Deep South was short and brutish. The day started before dawn, when the overseer sounded the horn. In the slave quarters, men, women and children scrambled up from mounds of straw piled on the mud floors of their tiny huts. Hoes in hand, they headed to the fields to plant, cultivate or harvest the crops.

At ten o'clock they were allowed a short break to build fires and cook breakfast. Most made hoecakes by mixing a little cornmeal with water and baking it over the fire on the blades of their hoes. Then it was back to work.

54

All day the overseer rode up and down the fields. He snapped a long cowhide whip to keep them too scared to talk back or revolt. He flogged anyone who wasn't working hard enough.

After a short break in the afternoon, the slaves worked until dark. Finally, after about 15 hours of hot, backbreaking labor, they were allowed to return to their huts to cook their evening meal. Into a pot of boiling cornmeal they might throw some greens from the tiny gardens many cultivated. And once a week, they would be given a little salt pork or fish. Then they crawled under quilts pieced together from scraps of leftover fabric and slept until the overseer's horn woke them to another day of labor.

Sunday was the only day of rest, the only day to wash clothes, tend their small vegetable patches and enjoy family life. On some plantations, the owner or his wife might arrange a church service for the slaves. Here, the stories they heard and the songs they sang brought a little comfort into lives marked by hard work and abuse.

THE COTTON GIN

Southern plantation owners had been growing cotton for decades before they found an efficient way to remove seeds and dirt from the cotton fibers. In 1793, a Georgia plantation owner, Mrs. Greene, was impressed with the many useful devices a visitor named Eli Whitney had invented for her household. She wondered if he could find a fast way to clean the cotton.

Within days Whitney had developed a machine simple enough to be built by the local blacksmith. He strung wires across the bottom of a box to make a grate. Circular saw blades that fit into the openings between the wires bit into the thick mass of raw cotton in the box, pulling the fibers through the grate and leaving seeds and dirt behind. Using this cotton gin (short for engine), one slave could clean 200 times more cotton than before.

Later Whitney added a waterwheel that turned 80 saws at a time. One gin now cleaned 1000 times more cotton a day. With mills in England and the northern states buying cotton as quickly as it could be shipped, people saw the chance for huge profits. Sadly, the growing demand for cotton meant more slaves were needed, too. Even though importing slaves from Africa had been made illegal in 1808, traders found ways to smuggle them in. As slaves became more valuable, harsher laws were passed to stop them from running away.

The cotton plant is a low-growing shrub. In its seed pods, called bolls, white fibers surround large seeds. When the fibers are dried and fluffed up, they can be twisted together to form a strong thread. Woven into cloth, cotton produces one of the cheapest and most useful fabrics in the world.

A FREED SLAVE

When Reuben was 15, he was whipped for arguing with the overseer. It was one of many floggings, but this time, as his back healed, he made plans to run away.

Freeing a slave was called manumission. Owners sometimes freed slaves, usually house slaves, in their wills. Others were bought and freed by abolitionists. Some slaves, whose owners allowed them to work for others in their spare time, even managed to buy their own freedom. Freed slaves always carried their papers to prove that they were no longer slaves.

Reuben's experience made him want to become a conductor on the Underground Railroad. He patrolled the riverbank at night, listening for runaways. He also left a lantern burning in the upstairs window as a coded message of welcome.

Runaways felt safest when their contacts were black like themselves. Although many white people acted as conductors or ran safe houses, the majority of the workers on the Underground Railroad were freed slaves and fugitives who decided to go back and rescue family and friends.

One of the safe houses along his route was Henry's tinsmith shop. Henry gave him refuge and work, but they were both worried about the slave catchers. Finally Henry decided there was only one way to keep Reuben safe. He bought Reuben from his master and then set him free.

THE SWAMP GHOST

Many slaves had to make their way through treacherous swamps filled with snakes and, in some cases, alligators. Ben had heard stories about the swamps. By far the scariest stories were about the swamp ghosts, spirits that traveled in eerie balls of fire or in dancing flickers of light. The spirits were just a superstition, but the swamp lights really existed.

As the water level rises in swamps and marshes, grasses and other plants are submerged and begin to rot. This rotting releases gasses, including methane. A strong concentration of methane can burst into flames. This may happen spontaneously or during a lightning storm. The burning gas is usually seen as flickering lights darting through the trees — a spooky sight that led to stories about supernatural spirits. The spirit thought to live in the fire was called will-o'-the-wisp, ignis fatuus or jack-o'-lantern.

BOLD ESCAPES

Most slaves escaped from slavery the way the Jacksons did, by running away at night, then following the North Star. Even if they were lucky enough to meet up with a conductor to take them on the Underground Railroad, they still needed stamina, courage and determination to make the long, long walk to Canada. Some fugitives, however, found ways to make the trip shorter and safer — although not always more comfortable.

Henry Brown, a slave living in Richmond, Virginia, had white friends who helped him construct a cloth-padded wooden crate. He settled inside it with a store of biscuits and a water bottle made from an animal bladder (a common way to make watertight bottles in those days). Then his friends nailed down the lid and shipped him to abolitionist friends in the free city of Philadelphia, Pennsylvania. The train journey took 26 hours. From then on he was known as "Box" Brown.

Runaways were hidden in a variety of containers. One small child was smuggled across the Detroit River to Windsor, Canada West (now Ontario), in the domed lid of a trunk. Many slaves spent part of their journeys crouching inside barrels or lying flat out in coffins, arriving at their destinations nearly suffocated.

Disguises were often used. Slave catchers watching for ragged fugitives wouldn't look twice at a "Quaker lady." The deep brim on a Quaker bonnet could easily hide the face of a male or female runaway. A short man and a tall woman might exchange clothes to confuse pursuers. A much bolder disguise was adopted by Ellen Craft, who escaped with her husband from Georgia. She was tall and had a light complexion. Dressed in a top hat and elegant suit she could pass as a southern planter. Her husband, William, posed as her personal servant. Because Ellen Craft couldn't read or write, she bandaged her right hand and carried it in a sling to avoid having to sign the guest register in hotels.

One conductor on the Underground Railroad led a group of 28 fugitives north. To disguise the group as they moved through a city, he created a mock funeral procession. Some of the group rode in the coach while others walked behind as mourners. Slave hunters looking for a group of 28 saw not only the wrong number, but also the wrong clothing.

Quick, bold escapes were not easy to organize. They required money and sympathetic friends. The only hope for most slaves was the slow, dangerous walk north.

Put a Lantern in the Window

Ben hunkered down behind a bush watching the house beyond the picket fence. It was in darkness except for the light in one upstairs window. His stomach knotted. Should he knock on that door or not? Look for the lantern, Momma had said. But what if she was wrong?

Can't wait forever, Ben thought, as the sky began to lighten. Gathering all his courage, he crept up to the door and knocked. It opened a crack.

"Welcome, friend," said a soft voice.

With a thankful sigh, Ben slipped in.

Putting a lantern in an upstairs window was an Underground Railroad signal. It meant safety, food and help were available. You can make a lantern similar to the one Reuben and Henry shone in their window to welcome Ben.

You'll need:
- a clean, empty tin can with one end removed
- a felt-tip marker
- an old towel
- a hammer
- nails of different sizes
- wire
- a short candle
- matches

1. Fill the can with water and place it in the freezer. Leave it overnight or until the water is frozen solid. The ice will give you a hard surface against which to hammer your pattern.

2. Use the marker to draw a simple design on the can.

3. Lay the can on its side on a folded towel. Using various sizes of nails, hammer the design into the can.

4. For the handle, hammer a hole on either side of the can near the top.

5. Loosen the ice with hot water and remove it. Dry the can. Thread the wire through the handle holes and bend the ends up. Be careful not to cut your hands on sharp edges.

6. Have an adult light the candle and drip a few drops of wax into the can. Blow out the candle and stand the candle upright in the wax. Let the wax harden.

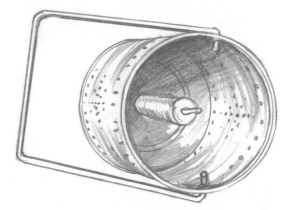

7. Ask an adult to light the candle, then watch the punched design throw a pattern onto the walls in a dark room.

OUTSIDERS

Johanna crumpled a sheet of newspaper and carefully stuffed it inside the glass chimney of the lamp. Soot smeared the back of her hand. Wiping it down the already smudged front of her pinafore, she sighed. No matter how careful she was, the black film got all over everything.

Across the table, four sparkling lamp chimneys sat in front of Eliza. She's as fussy as Mother, Johanna thought crossly. And if she doesn't stop that humming . . . Grinding her teeth, Johanna turned to look out the window. The rain had stopped at last. Two days they'd all been cooped up together. Two days of Eliza's irritating willingness. Can I help you with this, missus? Can I help you with that, missus? And those reproving looks from Mother. Why aren't you as helpful, Johanna, they seemed to say.

"Look!" Eliza said, and Johanna turned back from the window. Eliza ran one finger around the inside rim of a lamp chimney, gathering up the lampblack. On the sheet of newsprint she traced a sprawling *E* followed by a lopsided *l*. "I can write my name."

"Everyone can write," Johanna snapped.

Eliza's grin faded. "*We* can't." She dashed the palm of her hand across the paper, smudging the letters. "Asked how once. Missus said I'd better not ask again or she'd give me what for."

"Then how *did* you learn?"

"The littlest missy. She loved scratchin' away at her slate. Doin' her alphabets, she called it." As she talked, Eliza traced her name again. Carefully she dotted the *i*, then sat back to look at it, smiling. "One day I says, 'Draw *my* name.' And she did. Then she made it on a piece of paper. Kept it in my pocket so's I could practice at it — way off from the house, in the sand down by the river. Tramped all over the marks after. So's no one would find 'em." She dipped her finger in the soot again.

Johanna thought about the hours hunched over her desk at school, her paper splotched with ink blots and tears as she made circles and sticks, circles and sticks. Mrs. Halley had been quick to smack her ruler across any hand that couldn't write neatly. Johanna had often gone home with red knuckles and redder eyes. "If it was so much trouble, why did you bother?"

Eliza stared at her in surprise, then looked back at the spidery letters that spelled her name. "I like the shape of it. I like the way it starts all curly. Then there's this shout," she retraced the *l*, "and it goes all whispery at the end. When I look at it scratched out like that, I can say — that's me. Eliza. A real person."

Later that day, when she was sweeping up the wood curls from the shop floor, Johanna complained to her father. "Yes, missus this, and yes, missus that, and, Papa, she can't even write — except for her name."

"That's not her fault, you know, Johanna," her father chided gently. "Owners keep their slaves ignorant to control them. I believe they even have a law forbidding anyone to teach slaves to read or write."

Johanna dumped a dustpanful of wood curls into the barrel used for tinder, then tried again. "Mother wants us to be friends but how can we be? We don't have anything in common."

"It's only for a few more days. Once we hear from Mr. Fuller, we'll know what to do." Johanna heard the impatience in his voice and swallowed her next complaint. Oh well, she thought, he's right. She won't be here forever.

But the truth was she felt all jangly — watching her tongue and being pleasant every minute of the day and never having time alone. So when her mother announced she needed a few things from the store, Johanna felt like a bird released from a cage. "Two spools of thread and some cotton tape," she sang as she skipped out the door. The dry goods store was in the center of town. She was sure to see some of her friends.

Johanna hadn't walked ten minutes before she spotted Suzanne and Rachel. "Wait up," she called as she ran to overtake them. Just what she'd been hoping for, a chance to catch up on the news, especially the plans for the garden party next Sunday. In the flurry about Eliza and Ben it had gone clear out of her mind. With a sudden pang, she thought, We will be able to go, won't we? Surely we won't have to stay home just because *they're* here.

The girls stopped to wait for Johanna, each swinging a small market basket. She arrived beside them, out of breath and with a stitch in her side.

"It's been such ages since I've seen you. I was just thinking about the garden party." She turned to Suzanne. "Is your father still going to drive us?" The whole town had been invited to a strawberry tea on the grounds of Rodman Hall. But the six girls who had just graduated from Mrs. Halley's School For Young Ladies had a special treat planned — a ride in Mr. Blakely's new carriage.

Rachel darted a look at Suzanne, then began searching earnestly through her basket. Suzanne's cheeks turned red. "Well, I . . . The truth of the matter is, Johanna — "

"He won't take us?"

"No. No, he's still taking us, but we thought . . . that is, Caroline suggested . . . "

Caroline! Not Caroline again! At school it was always Caroline who directed their games, ordering this one here and that one there.

"She suggested what?"

"Well, she pointed out — and I guess I have to agree with her — there isn't really room for six in the barouche, not without crushing our skirts, and since your family is sure to be going in your father's wagon, we decided . . . "

"Decided what?"

"Perhaps you should go with your family. After all," Suzanne rushed on, "it doesn't matter how we get there, as long as we all arrive." She stopped abruptly. "I . . . I have to go now. My mother said I was to bring this ribbon straight home to her."

Johanna clamped her teeth together to stop her chin from trembling. Not for the world would she let Suzanne and Rachel see how hurt she was. As they scuttled down the street, she took several deep breaths to calm herself.

She turned and slowly walked the last few blocks to Dunsmore's Dry Goods. As she entered, the door flew out of her hand and banged against the wall. Heads lifted and turned. One of them was Caroline's.

Caroline had been inspecting a bolt of pink calico. She pursed her lips as though considering buying it, then glanced sideways at Johanna.

"I hear you have guests." Her trick of emphasizing the last word in a sentence always sounded slightly sneering.

"Where did you hear that?"

"Who knows where these little snippets come from? But I'm sure everyone's heard. So hard to keep a secret in this town."

Johanna felt her face going red. She had never been good at deflecting Caroline's catty remarks. And what exactly did Caroline mean by "guests"? Was she just fishing, or did she know about Eliza and Ben?

"Of course, one must be charitable," the high, cool voice persisted. "Mama always contributes to the clothing drive for them. But to have such people right in your house, Johanna. Mama thinks it so peculiar. Just not done in our circle, she says."

So that was it. Indignation rose sourly in Johanna's throat. Before hot words could spill out, Caroline had turned and was walking away. Over her shoulder, as she swept toward the door, she added, "By the way, has Suzanne mentioned to you — about the barouche? Quite ridiculous really for all six of us to squeeze in. I'm sure you understand."

Johanna gritted her teeth. "I understand perfectly, Caroline. Perfectly."

As the door snapped shut, Johanna had to reach for the counter to steady herself. How dare Caroline! And Suzanne agreed with her! Had let Caroline talk her into excluding Johanna! Forget it. Forget it until you get home, she told herself, suddenly aware of inquiring looks from people she should be greeting politely.

Back out on the road, her mother's parcels tucked into her basket, Johanna let angry tears spill over. She had daydreamed about the ride to the garden party for weeks — the six of them all in new dresses, with parasols to match, leaning over the elegant sweep of the carriage sides, waving to their neighbors.

Caroline's smile floated before her, so tightly sweet, so poisonous. She's not our kind, really, she could almost hear Caroline murmuring to Suzanne. Her father's only a cooper. And now her family is taking in slaves.

Snobs, Johanna thought. Stuck-up snobs. Who cares? Then she thought of the garden party again. If only we hadn't . . . She stopped herself. If only we hadn't taken in Eliza and Ben? Did she really mean that?

Johanna thought about the stories Eliza had told. About fleeing from tracking dogs and walking down the street right under the noses of the slave catchers, yes, but those other stories, too. Like the day Eliza was told she couldn't play with the master's children anymore. She was six and old enough to work in the kitchen, the mistress had decided. Or the way she'd been forbidden to learn her letters because she was only a slave.

Nobody should be left out like that, Johanna thought, tears welling up again. Well, there's nothing I can do about it. She trudged along, not caring who saw her tear-stained cheeks. Then a thought struck her so forcibly that she stopped right in the middle of the road. I *can* do something. I can.

And then she was running pell-mell toward their gate. As she burst through the kitchen door, her mother and Eliza looked up from the beans they were cutting.

"What on earth is the matter?" her mother asked.

Johanna yanked open the drawer of the dish dresser. Scrabbling under neatly ironed tea towels, she pulled out her school slate, a speller and her First Reader.

"Eliza," she turned to the girl staring wide-eyed at her, "how would you like to learn to read?"

Eliza swallowed. "Read?" she whispered. She sat very still, her gaze grave and questioning. "If I could read," she started slowly, then suddenly her face lit up. "If I could read, I could do anything!"

FREEDOM TO READ AND WRITE

By the time Eliza was born, most southern states had passed laws forbidding anyone to teach a slave to read and write. Because of that, on her flight to freedom, Eliza couldn't consult a map, check the names of towns and streets on signs, read a train timetable or recognize her description on a wanted poster. Running away was difficult for slaves who couldn't read, and that was just what slave owners wanted. Slaves who couldn't read books or newspapers seldom came in contact with new ideas that might make them question their bondage or lead them to revolt against their owners.

People who disobeyed the law and educated their slaves were sent to jail. Despite the law, some slaves did learn to read and write. Most learned from overhearing the owners' children at their lessons or were taught by the children themselves. And education *did* make them discontented with their lives. Many educated slaves became preachers and teachers, passing on new ideas, encouraging their fellow slaves to think for themselves.

FREDERICK DOUGLASS

Frederick Douglass risked his life to speak out against the practice of not educating black people. As a child in Maryland, he was taught to read by his owner's wife. Since this was against the law, the woman's husband ordered her to stop. But even that little bit of education made Frederick question his life as a slave. For asking questions he was beaten regularly.

At 21, he managed to escape and took the last name of Douglass. He began speaking at antislavery meetings about his life. His speeches were powerful enough to sway people to the abolitionist cause. In Rochester, New York, he started a newspaper called the *North Star*, in which he promised black people that he would "fearlessly assert your rights" and "faithfully proclaim your wrongs."

He also urged them to work hard for an education and the right to vote.

Frederick Douglass used his home as a station on the Underground Railroad. Many escaped slaves hid safely in its secret rooms until he was able to get them across Lake Ontario to Canada. Eventually his work attracted powerful enemies. When a warrant was issued for his arrest, he was forced to flee to Canada himself. Based in St. Catharines for a few months in 1859, he continued to write and speak against slavery. Many people who defended slavery claimed that black people were too childlike to educate. Frederick Douglass, through his life and work, proved that all they needed was the opportunity to learn.

STORYTELLING

Slaves who couldn't read or write handed on their history, hopes and fears through storytelling and song.

Even though African people spoke different languages, the stories they brought with them had many elements in common. Some tried to explain how things began: why the sun seemed to rise in the east and set in the west, how people first got fire. Some told of heroes and heroines who performed great deeds. Many were animal tales that used humor to help children remember important lessons.

As they told one another stories around the campfire at night or in the dark of their small cabins, the slaves gradually changed the stories to suit their new land. In Africa, animal stories were told about Elephant, Lion, Python and Spider. In America, the animals were changed to such local animals as Bear, Fox, Raccoon and Rabbit. To show respect, the storyteller called the animals Sister, Brother, Aunt or Uncle. In one well-known tale about Brer (Brother) Rabbit, a little animal outsmarts a bigger, stronger animal, a message of hope and comfort for people who had to use their wits to survive.

Brer Rabbit and Tar Baby

Brer Fox was hungry. Rabbit stew, he thought, and his mouth watered. I'll have me some rabbit stew. Now, Brer Fox had tried time and again to catch Brer Rabbit, but Brer Rabbit always tricked him and got away.

This time, thought Brer Fox, I'll get him for sure. He took some tar, mixed it with turpentine and formed it into the shape of a baby. He set a hat on Tar Baby and put her down beside the road. Pretty soon along came Brer Rabbit — lippity-clippity, clippity-lippity.

Brer Fox lay low.

Brer Rabbit spied Tar Baby. "Morning!" he said politely, but Tar Baby just sat there and Brer Fox lay low.

"Nice weather this morning." Brer Rabbit thought he'd give her one more chance, but Tar Baby said nothing and Brer Fox just lay low.

Now, Brer Rabbit had a temper and he didn't like to be ignored. "You deaf?" he said. "'Cause if you is, I can holler!"

But Tar Baby never moved and Brer Fox still lay low.

"You're stuck up, that's what," said Brer Rabbit. "Well, I'll cure you of that." And blip! he whacked her on the side of the head. His fist stuck firm and he couldn't pull loose.

Brer Fox chuckled to himself and Tar Baby just sat still.

"If you don't loose me, I'll biff you again!" hollered Brer Rabbit. And *blip*! he whacked her with the other hand. It stuck fast. Tar Baby said nothing but Brer Fox could hardly keep himself down.

"Let go!" hollered Brer Rabbit, kicking Tar Baby. Pretty soon both feet and his head were stuck fast.

Then out popped Brer Fox looking as innocent as a mockingbird. "Howdy, Brer Rabbit. You look all stuck up this morning." And he rolled on the ground and laughed and laughed. "I got you this time, Brer Rabbit. You been running around sassing me for a long time, but this time you's come to the end of the row. I'm going to build a brushfire and boil you up in a stew."

Now, Brer Rabbit knew he was in trouble, so he kept his voice soft and humble. "Boil me up all you want, Brer Fox, but please, don't fling me into that briar patch."

Brer Fox looked at the briar patch and then at Brer Rabbit. "Too much trouble to boil you up," he said. "I'll just roast you over the fire."

"Roast me all you want, Brer Fox, but please, please, don't fling me into that briar patch."

Brer Fox thought about gathering up all that wood. "Too much trouble to roast you," he said. "I'll just stomp on you."

"Stomp on me all you want, Brer Fox, but please, please, please, don't fling me into that briar patch."

Brer Fox thought back to all the times Brer Rabbit had tricked him. He looked at Brer Rabbit crouched shivering on the ground, then he looked at the briar patch.

"Hee, hee, Brer Rabbit," he said, "I'll fix you." And he grabbed him by one leg and flung him as hard as he could right into the middle of that prickly, spiny briar patch. Then Brer Fox sat down to see what would happen.

By and by he heard someone calling. Way up the hill sat Brer Rabbit, combing tar out of his fur. "Hee, hee, Brer Fox," he called out. "I was born and bred in a briar patch. Born and bred!"

Share a Story

Eliza's favorite time on the plantation came when the day's work was done. Often, after supper was cooked and eaten, the slaves gathered around a fire or in the dark of a cabin to share stories. One person might turn a personal adventure into a tale, another might retell a story heard from a grandmother. In this way they passed on the history and wisdom of the tribe.

We all belong to tribes — our families, our schoolmates, our camp friends. With each group we have a shared history, shared stories. You can turn something you have experienced into a story to tell aloud, or you can look in collections of folktales and fairy-tales for old stories to retell. Here are some tips to make your story come alive:

1. Read or say the story out loud at least twice to practice. As you read, try to visualize what is happening in the story.

2. Organize the story in your mind by listing five or six important steps that move the story forward. This makes a framework for remembering the story. The framework for Brer Rabbit looks like this:
   - Fox wants Rabbit for dinner.
   - Fox makes Tar Baby and waits.
   - Rabbit comes along and talks to Tar Baby.
   - Rabbit gets mad and hits Tar Baby.
   - Fox appears and decides to cook Rabbit.
   - Rabbit tricks Fox and gets away.

74

3. Think of action words to brighten up the story. For example, instead of "throw" you could use "fling" or "pitch."

4. Look for places to add sound effects, such as different voices for the main characters or words that imitate sounds and feelings. For example, a snake might use words that start with *s*. Drag them out to imitate hissing.

5. Rehearse. Practice telling the story but don't memorize it. Be chatty. Try to sound as though you're talking to friends. It's all right if the story changes a little with each telling.

6. Watch yourself in a mirror as you practice. Experiment with hand gestures and facial expressions that emphasize the mood of the story.

7. Use your voice to add interest to your story. Speak much more slowly than usual. Change your tone from loud to soft and from high to low at appropriate times in the story. Pause just before an exciting moment.

8. Create a special setting for your story. Choose a quiet place with few distractions. Your audience should be sitting comfortably, either on chairs or on the ground. To create a dreamlike place, turn the lights down (or off for a ghost story). Some storytellers start by lighting a candle.

9. Pay attention to how you begin and end. Gather your listeners' attention with phrases such as "Once upon a time," "Long ago and far away" or "In the far-off days when animals could talk." At the end, release your audience from the story with such phrases as "And that's how . . . came to be," or "Snip, snap, snout, my tale's told out."

SLAVE CATCHER!

Johanna opened the back door to the cooperage and breathed in deeply. She liked to stand for a minute and let the smells surround her. The scent of fresh wood told her that her father and Tom were planing. As she stepped into the room, Tom's head came up, and the zip, zip of his plane stopped. No need to tell *him* it was dinnertime. He was already brushing the wood shavings from his leather apron.

At the front of the shop her father was smoothing the rim of a half-finished barrel, one eye on a thin-faced man whose elbows were planted on the display counter. Something about him made Johanna duck back into the shadows.

"Nice work y'do here," the stranger drawled. "See ya got a wagonload a' barrels out there 'bout ready to go." The only answer was the vroop, vroop of the palm-sized plane.

"Been havin' a good look 'round yer town," the man continued. "Reckon on stayin' awhile." As he spoke, his sharp eyes searched the room, stopping for a moment at the door to the house, then moving on to the wall piled high with barrels. "Fact is," he persisted, "gonna be needing some hired help. Pay a good wage to a young girl fer a bit a' cookin' and cleanin'. Some sewin' maybe. You know of any might be lookin' fer work?"

Mr. Reid eased the tilted barrel upright until it rested flat on the floor, then looked the man square in the eyes. "This is a cooper's shop. You want a hired girl, you'll have to look elsewhere."

Johanna felt her chest tighten. Her father never spoke to customers in that terse voice. Why was he being so rude to this one?

"No offense, friend. Just thought I'd ask." The stranger peered intently around the shop again. "Y'never know where yer likely to find exactly what yer looking fer. Y'hear of any interested party . . . " He paused with his hand on the doorknob. "I'd be obliged." And he sidled out.

Johanna felt a sick thud in her stomach as the door clicked shut. "Papa, what if he's — "

"Now, Johanna, no sense speculating," her father interrupted. "We'll just wait and see. Meanwhile, it's dinnertime, is it?" He glanced toward the back of the shop. Tom had already left. "And don't go worrying your mother about this, my girl. No need to borrow trouble."

Later, as they were finishing dinner, Mr. Reid said, "Tom and I are away to Queenston this afternoon with that load of barrels for Abram Fuller. So I want you to stay clear of the windows, Eliza, and scoot upstairs if anyone comes to call. We've no reason to think anything's amiss but we'd best keep on the safe side a few days longer."

"Better safe than sorry," Mrs. Reid agreed, then added, "After the dishes are done, you girls can finish making up those berry boxes. We'll be needing them soon."

Strawberry time, Johanna thought with a pang. She'd been looking forward to the strawberry tea for months and now the thought of seeing those stuck-up girls made her feel sick.

Eliza was singing softly as she set out the thin sheets of wood Tom had planed for them in the cooper's shop. "Freedom train's a-comin'. I see it close at hand. I hear the wheels a-rumblin' . . . " Eliza made her voice deep and grumbly and Johanna laughed.

"Get on board, little children, get on board . . . " Johanna joined in. Eliza had been singing nonstop since Ben had arrived. Even though he'd been sent off to Johanna's uncle so there wouldn't seem to be too much unusual activity at the Reids', Eliza was happy as a cricket. "There's room for many a-more," she sang out.

The girls had berry baskets stacked so high they were wobbling when a sharp rap came at the kitchen door. Scooping up the last of the unfolded strips, they darted into the small bedroom off the kitchen. Johanna listened at the door for a moment, then whispered, "That's my sister Jane's hired girl. What on earth can she be wanting?"

Mrs. Reid came bustling in. "I must go! Jane's baby has come down with spotted fever. I don't like leaving you two alone but Jane's frantic."

"We'll be fine," Johanna said. "You go along. We'll just sit in here and finish the boxes."

Reassured, Mrs. Reid set out for her older daughter's house.

The girls folded the boxes in silence. "I've got a splinter," Johanna said finally. She sucked at her index finger. "Let's have tea. You stay in here. I'll get it."

"Get on board . . . get on board . . . ," she hummed, clattering mugs and muffin tins onto the kitchen table. As she turned to lift the kettle off the stove, a movement outside the window caught her eye. Was it just a shadow, that tall, weedy shape? Suddenly a face peered in at her. Johanna's heart lurched into her mouth as the face grinned, then disappeared. The man from the shop!

She flew toward the door. Before she could bolt it shut, the handle turned and the door swung open. Without so much as a "by your leave," the man stepped into the kitchen.

"Yes?" she asked sharply. "What do you want?"

"Afternoon, missy." A thin-lipped smile stretched his stubbly cheeks. "Got some real good news fer yer little guest."

Johanna's quick glance toward the bedroom brought a glint of triumph to the man's eyes. His smile broadened to show crooked, yellow teeth. "Got a message from her ma." He raised his voice. "She's safe here in Canada and wants her little girl to come right away."

Standing firmly in his way, Johanna frowned. "You didn't say anything to my father about that this morning."

He raised his eyebrows and shrugged. "Didn't know the little lady existed this morning. Just met my good friend Abram Fuller on the road. Soon's I heard what he was about, I said, 'Don't you trouble yerself. I'll be right in that neighborhood. Be pleased to pass on the joyful news and bring ya the little girl myself.'" He grinned at her again. "Now just fetch out yer little friend and we'll be on our way."

"You're mistaken. There's no one else here."

The stranger's face flushed red. "You fetch me that girl — now!"

Terrified, Johanna turned to run. He caught her by the wrist but she twisted wildly and bit down hard on the hand that held her.

"Thunderation!" he spat, and let go just as Eliza swept out of the bedroom. Head down, she charged full tilt into the stranger, butting him so hard that he staggered backward, tripped on the doorstep and sprawled full-length on the porch. Johanna jumped for the door, slammed it shut and shot both bolts.

Weak with relief, the girls stared at each other.

"A slave catcher?"

Eliza nodded.

"How do you know?"

Eliza shrugged. "A feelin'. Just knows about folk like that. Anyways, what call's Mist' Fuller got to send him here? He knows your daddy's bringin' him barrels today."

Johanna sank limply onto a chair, but Eliza stood in the middle of the room, listening tensely. "What's he at now?"

Johanna tiptoed to the window. To her horror, the slave catcher was standing in the yard, staring at the roof.

"He's still out there. He's not going away," she said, half turning to Eliza. But when she looked again, he had vanished. She imagined him prowling around the house, searching, searching. There was no way in at the back. The shop would be locked and the lean-to had only one small window, though there was another window along the side of the shop. Surely he wouldn't dare try the front door. Anyway, it was locked — wasn't it? She raced into the parlor, Eliza at her heels.

Yes, it was locked. As an added precaution, Johanna shot the bolts, then checked the door that led from the parlor to the lean-to.

As she latched it firmly, she said, "Perhaps we should make a run for it. Mother's just down the road. The neighbors might hear us if we screamed." And then again they mightn't. The houses were far apart here on the outskirts of St. Catharines.

Eliza clutched at Johanna and pointed. A shadow passed in front of the window. The front door handle rattled briefly, then the shadow flitted across the next window.

"He's circling the house," Johanna whispered. "Listen, Eliza, as soon as he's around the back, head out the front door."

"How'll we know he's out back? Could be he's just ready n' waitin' to pounce. Better we wait right here. Long as he's outside, we're safe inside."

"*Shhh*!" Johanna said. "What was that?"

From somewhere came the crash of breaking glass. The girls stood rigid, straining to hear. The house was silent. A sudden thud made them start. Then a door hinge creaked.

"He's broken into the shop!" Johanna gasped. A loud bang and a sharp oath exploding into the silence told her the intruder had stumbled over something in the lean-to. Now only the flimsy parlor door with its hook-and-eye latch barred his way.

"We've *got* to run for it!" Johanna gasped, but Eliza was already tugging at the lower bolt on the front door. Johanna threw herself at the upper one, willing her mind to concentrate, to blot out the sounds of the blows that were shattering the parlor door. With a lurch, the bolt yielded. Now the key. Just as the big teeth tripped the lock, the back door splintered open.

"Run! Run!" Johanna screamed, pushing Eliza out in front of her. As they sped down the front steps, Johanna felt a hand on her shoulder, twisted out from under it and darted after Eliza. They turned into the road. Johanna raced ahead. Sprinting to catch up, Eliza stumbled in a wagon rut and fell.

"Gotcha!"

Johanna whirled around as the slave catcher dragged Eliza roughly to her feet. She ran at the man, pummeling him with her fists. "Let go. Let go. Let go!"

Her screams were drowned out by the thudding of horses' hooves and the clatter of wagon wheels. The slave catcher pushed Eliza away so suddenly that both girls fell onto the muddy road. As Johanna struggled to her knees, she saw her brother jump from the still-moving wagon right onto the fleeing slave catcher. Both crashed to the ground, rolling over and over. By the time Johanna was on her feet, her father had managed to halt the team. Neighbors came running. In no time a small knot of women huddled by the road, gawking as Tom pinned one arm behind the man's back and swung him around.

Mr. Reid seized the slave catcher by his lapels and glared into his face. "Listen, my friend." He was almost whispering with rage. "In this town we don't take kindly . . . to anyone terrorizing . . . our children. Neither do we like vermin . . . who traffic . . . in the slave trade. If you value your hide . . . you won't show your face . . . on this side of the river . . . again!"

After the last shake, he whirled the slave catcher around and, with a mighty shove between the shoulder blades, propelled him down the road. The man staggered for a few steps before he realized that he was free. Then he broke into a trot, stumbling from time to time as he glowered back over his shoulder at them.

Mr. Reid gathered both girls into his arms.

"You should have seen him go flying," Johanna said, "when Eliza butted him in the stomach."

Eliza smiled, but the sight of the slave catcher, shaking a defiant fist at them, made her say, "What if he comes back?"

"We'll set watchers, for him and any friends he's brought along." Mr. Reid sounded grim. "If he comes back, we'll be ready."

Yes, thought Johanna, whatever happens, Eliza and I will be ready, too.

SLAVE CATCHERS

W"hy does she have to hide?" Johanna had asked the day she discovered Eliza in the sewing room.

Her mother looked troubled. "Things happen," she said. "More than we ever hear about."

Even in the safety of Canada, ex-slaves had to be constantly on the lookout. In 1830 Charles Baby hired Andrew, an escaped slave, to work on his farm near Windsor. Andrew's owner traced him to Canada and sent five men to kidnap him. They rowed across the Detroit River on a Sunday morning, hoping to catch Andrew working alone in a field. Charles saw them and called on his neighbors to help drive off the men. Andrew's near capture showed that he was not safe close to the border so Charles gave him money to go to Toronto.

In many other cases citizens, both black and white, rescued escaping slaves from pursuers. But the danger remained. In 1853, a young boy was grabbed by slave catchers on the streets of Chatham, Canada West (now Ontario). Black journalist Mary Ann Shadd heard his cries, snatched him from the kidnappers and ran with him to the courthouse, where she rang the bell to alert the townsfolk. When people realized what was happening, they chased the kidnappers out of town.

Because slavery was against the law in Canada, slave hunters who followed fugitives across the border often used guile rather than force. Some pretended to hire escaped slaves as servants. Using this trick, the slave catchers lured them back into the United States, where they were held in jail until their owners came for them.

Why did the slave catchers go to so much trouble? Money! Slaves were so valuable that owners offered large rewards for the return of their "property." As a skilled seamstress and cook, Leah Jackson could be sold for $1000 or hired out to earn money for her owner. Ben and Eliza were young and had many years of hard work in them. The owner might post rewards of $500 for each one — a strong temptation back when $400 was a year's salary for a teacher.

The money attracted violent men. In the United States, slave catchers used dogs and guns to track down runaways. Because a dead fugitive was worth nothing, the slave catchers loaded their guns with bird shot, which would merely wound, not kill their quarry. One clever fugitive lined a vest with pouches stuffed with turkey feathers — an early version of the bulletproof vest.

Slave catchers were also unscrupulous. They didn't care if they found the actual slave described on a wanted poster as long as they were paid the money. As a result, free black people were often abducted and sold into slavery. In Canada, because the greatest danger lay near the border, many fugitives headed inland to such places as St. Catharines or Toronto, where an active abolitionist society kept watch. But the large rewards made slave catchers bold. Until 1863, when slavery was abolished in the United States, all black people, free or escaped slaves, had to be wary and vigilant every moment of the day.

ALEXANDER ROSS

Escaping slaves must have wondered if any white person could be trusted, and yet many white people went to extraordinary lengths to help runaways. Alexander Ross, a doctor from Belleville, Canada West (now Ontario), spent much time and money helping slaves escape. He grew up in a family concerned with helping the downtrodden in society. When he read Harriet Beecher Stowe's *Uncle Tom's Cabin,* he saw it as "a command . . . to help the oppressed to freedom."

To see for himself the life that slaves led, Dr. Ross traveled through the southern States. He used his interest in bird-watching as an excuse to ask slave owners for permission to roam through their fields and woodlands. On these outings he made contact with slaves, inviting them to secret meetings where he gave detailed information about escape routes to Canada. Slaves who decided to escape were given money, a compass, a knife and some food. On occasion, Dr. Ross led the runaways all the way to Canada himself. One woman made the trip disguised as his valet.

Alexander Ross never stopped reaching out to the oppressed. Once he had helped the black community establish itself in Canada, he turned his attention to the problems of Native people.

SONGS

"Momma, she sings all the time," Eliza said when Johanna asked how she knew so many songs. "Keeps you workin', keeps you happy, she says. But sometimes, at night, her singin's mighty sad."

Slaves hoeing in the fields under the blistering sun or hefting bales of cotton onto riverboats used music to lighten the burden of their work. They were forbidden to play the drums of their native Africa because these could be used to communicate with other groups of slaves. But they worked the old rhythms into their new songs. Taking words from the Bible stories they heard in the plantation chapels on Sundays, they sang about Jonah in the belly of the whale, Elijah and the great wheel of fire, and the hardships of Hebrew slaves in Egypt struggling to reach the Promised Land. These spirituals, as they were called, gave hope and comfort to a people who toiled in a hard and unrewarding life.

Go Down, Moses

Get on Board

Get on board, lit – tle chil – dren, get on board, lit – tle

chil – dren, Get on board, lit – tle chil – dren, there's room for ma – ny a - more.

Auction Block

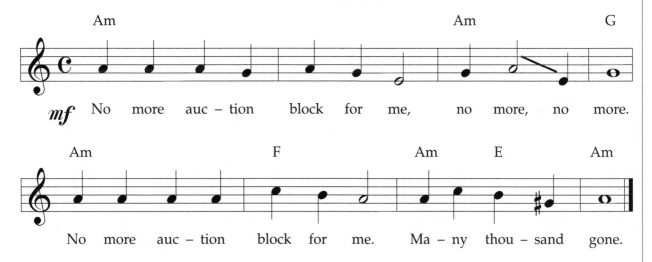

mf No more auc – tion block for me, no more, no more.

No more auc – tion block for me. Ma – ny thou – sand gone.

FRIENDS

"J-O-H-A-N-N-A." Eliza's finger traced the letters running across a framed picture on the parlor wall. "It says Johanna! You sewed your name onto this."

"Yes. It's a sampler — a way to practice letters and sewing at the same time. Mine isn't very good. I got tired of doing it after I stitched the alphabet and my name and the date. Look at my mother's." Johanna pointed to a large framed sampler on the next wall. "She was only six and she did a Bible verse and everything. Here, I'll read it to you."

"Let me. Let *me*!" But the tiny cross-stitches and unusual words were too much for Eliza's shaky reading skills. She was practicing every spare minute, copying words onto the slate or reading from Johanna's First Reader. She had even stuck to her lessons now that Ben was back at the Reids'. He was learning to read, too. Ben was keen but Eliza was tireless.

"I used to watch the little missies do their letters and I knew, I just *knew*, if I could read, there'd be no difference between us."

Ben looked up from his slate. "Readin's good," he said slowly. "But folks'll still make a difference. Don't you go thinkin' otherwise."

Ben's warning bothered Johanna. She thought about the north end of St. Catharines. The neat, small houses crowded around the church where black people worshipped. Wasn't everyone supposed to be equal here? Most people were friendly, but once she'd seen Caroline and her mother pointedly cross the road and disappear into a shop rather than stop and talk to Orrin Brown. They were happy enough to have him mend their shoes, but to chat on the street . . .

After dinner the next day, Eliza asked to learn some everyday words. "Reader's fine," she said, "but I'd like to see what the words in my head look like." She scanned the list Johanna printed on a square of butcher's paper. Suddenly she went still, then copying carefully, scratched onto her slate, "My mother will come soon."

Johanna felt her heart contract. What if Mrs. Jackson never came? What would Eliza and Ben do? A large tear landed on the slate, blotting out "will," and Eliza's face crumpled. Then her shoulders were shaking and her head was buried in her arms on the table.

Johanna reached out and felt the thin body heave under great, gulping sobs. In a panic she shouted, "Mother! Mother!" She'd never seen anyone cry this hard.

96

Mrs. Reid came running. She took one look, scooped Eliza into her arms and began to rock her gently. "There, there," she said, stroking Eliza's head.

"Mist' Fuller promised . . . he promised," Eliza gasped. "But she's not comin', is she? I'll never see her again."

The door opened and Mr. Reid came into the room. He looked in alarm at Eliza and then at his wife.

"James, we must do something," she said. "Eliza and Ben can't live with this uncertainty any longer."

As they talked, Eliza crept out of Mrs. Reid's arms and sat erect on a kitchen chair, her hands folded tightly in her lap. "Sorry, missus," she said, scrubbing at a tear with one knuckle. "Didn't mean to be ungrateful."

Mrs. Reid reached out and clasped Eliza's hands. "You mustn't think that way, Eliza. We're glad to have you here. We just feel so helpless. We have no way of tracing your mother. We have to depend entirely on Mr. Fuller and his connections." She turned to her husband. "James . . ."

"I'll have Tom take a message to Abram Fuller. If there's any news at all about Mrs. Jackson, we must know. Then we can make plans about getting these children away to somewhere safer."

Johanna stared at her father. Eliza leave? Of course. The slave catcher had been run off, but who knew if he was gone for good. I don't want her to leave, Johanna thought, and was surprised at how strongly she felt.

Eliza had been listening carefully, too. "Oh thank you, missus," she said, jumping up to hug Mrs. Reid as the door closed behind Mr. Reid.

"Now, Eliza, please don't go getting your hopes up," Mrs. Reid warned. "There may well be no news." Or, Johanna thought, with a shiver, there may be bad news.

Eliza settled down to work again, reading out loud with a little prompting from Johanna. But after two pages, her voice faltered. She put down the reader. "Need to be up and doin'," she said. "Only thing stops me from thinkin' and worryin'."

"How about picking some strawberries?" Mrs. Reid suggested. "There should be enough for supper in the fence angles across the road. You're in view of the house from there. But take the dinner bell with you just in case."

Johanna opened her mouth to protest. They'd look ridiculous carrying a dinner bell. But the memory of the slave catcher made her think again. Silently she stowed the bell in the flat basket they used to cart the berry boxes.

"Three boxes will be plenty for supper," Mrs. Reid said. "Mind you put on your sunbonnets. It's hot today."

Eliza practically danced out the door. "Don't know if I should wear this pretty dress out in the fields," she said, smoothing down the blue gingham that Johanna had fetched for her from the blanket box that morning. Eliza's delight at the dress made Johanna feel doubly mean for keeping it back. Don't say it was my favorite dress, she thought when she saw her mother's look of surprise. "The apron will protect it," was all she said now.

They waved to Ben on the way out. He'd offered to load barrels onto the wagon. "Stay close by in the yard," Mr. Reid had warned him.

"Seems like forever since I was out," Eliza said as she followed Johanna across the road. "Smell that grass. Don't seem like anything bad could happen with the sun shinin' and the bees hummin'. Let's find them berries!"

"Should be lots along this fence. Let's try here." A cedar fence snaked between the road and a hayfield. The girls climbed the rails and dropped to the other side. "This field belongs to Suzanne's father, but he doesn't mind us picking his strawberries."

"Here's some!" Eliza crouched down and began picking.

"They always seem to hide themselves in the bends of the fence. Nice and sweet, these ones." Johanna worked one way along the fence and Eliza the other. In no time Johanna had a box full of the tiny berries. Some were so ripe they squashed as she touched them.

She was licking juice and berry pulp from her fingers when a voice called, "Hello! Can I come and pick with you?"

Johanna bobbed up to find Caroline peering over the fence.

"Oh!" Caroline's smile faded. "It's *you*." She looked down the fence line at the figure in blue gingham crouched some distance away. "I thought you were Suzanne. It *is* her father's field, after all."

Johanna glanced over her shoulder at Eliza. "You can come and pick if you like," she said. "Mr. Blakely won't mind, I'm sure."

Caroline hesitated, then clambered over the fence and started toward the stooping figure. "Suzanne?"

Eliza turned and lifted her sunbonneted face. Caroline stopped short. For one frozen moment, the two girls stared at each other, then Caroline whirled and marched away from the still crouching girl.

Johanna felt hot blood rush to her face. How dare she! Beckoning to Eliza to come closer, she stepped in front of Caroline, blocking her path. "Before you go, there's someone I'd like you to meet." She reached out to draw Eliza to her side and linked arms with her. "This is my friend, Eliza Jackson."

Caroline's eyes wavered. For once, she looked unsure of herself. Then her lips thinned into a hard line. Without a word, she turned and strode toward the fence, her bonnet flopping on its strings as she went.

Johanna turned to Eliza. "I'm so sorry . . . " But Eliza wasn't listening. She was smiling down at their linked arms.

Later, their boxes full, they wandered back to the house. "She gonna be mean to you 'cause of me?" Eliza asked.

Johanna thought of all the times she'd wanted so much to please Caroline. How often had she found herself swallowing arguments, giving in, doing things Caroline's way?

"Who cares?" Johanna was surprised to hear herself say.

They were sitting on the porch hulling strawberries when Tom rode into the yard.

Eliza's hands tightened on the bowl of berries. She looked at Johanna, then she smoothed down her pinafore and stood up. "No sense waitin' here, I reckon."

Ben appeared in the stable door. "Any news?" he called.

Without answering, Tom untied a cotton bag from the saddle and handed it to Eliza. She darted a quick look at Ben, then slowly pulled open the top.

Out of the bag she took a small figure made from twists and braids of cornhusking. It had been lovingly dressed in blue calico. "It's my doll! The very one my momma made for me." Pressing the doll to her chest, she turned to Tom.

He cleared his throat and then broke into a big grin. "Your mother's in Toronto," he said. "Safe and sound and waiting for you."

Over the next 24 hours they had hardly a moment to draw breath. Eliza and Ben were frantic to see their mother, and the Reids wanted them safely away from any slave catchers who might be lurking.

"Train's the fastest way," Mr. Reid said. "Besides, there might be watchers on the ferry at Port Dalhousie. Abram Fuller's sending his oldest son to ride with you, just to be on the safe side."

"Train?" Eliza's eyes were shining. "Never been on one of them before."

"Not the above-ground kind anyway," Johanna reminded her, and they both laughed.

Mrs. Reid found a small carpetbag in the attic and they packed the reader, speller and slate on the bottom, a change of clothes for Ben in the middle and, very carefully on top, the blue gingham dress. And all the while Eliza was singing, "Get on board, little children, get on board. There's room for many a-more."

I mustn't begrudge her this, Johanna thought. It's wonderful that she's going to be with her mother. But will she miss me as much as I'll miss her? All too soon, Johanna found herself standing on the railroad platform waving good-bye.

"Well, that's the end of that," she sighed, trailing upstairs a few hours later. The door of the sewing room stood ajar, just as it had the first time she'd seen Eliza. She gave it a small shove. The room was so tidy it was hard to believe anyone had lived there. Then she caught sight of the china doll and happiness swept through her. It sat, as prim as ever, in the middle of the neatly made cot. Resting against it, a calico arm tucked into the blue gingham one, was Eliza's cornhusk doll.

SIX MONTHS LATER

It was three days before Christmas when the parcel arrived. Johanna undid the string and opened one end. A letter was tucked underneath a square of linen. As she drew the linen out, it unfolded to reveal row on row of tiny, perfect cross-stitches. Around the edges, Eliza had worked a garland of the crimson hedge roses she would have seen the length of the Niagara Peninsula on her train ride to Toronto. The garland linked two names.

Johanna looked at the accompanying letter, her eyes almost too blurred by tears to read.

"My dearest friend," it began . . .

THE RESCUE

When slave catchers captured Eliza's mother, the Underground Railroad went into action. Coded messages alerted all agents in the area. Eyes and ears around the countryside soon located two men camping in the woods. They had tied Leah Jackson to a tree while they waited for her owner to arrive. Under cover of darkness, Underground Railroad agents snatched her away.

Once she was safely hidden, a coded message was sent by the new electric telegraph to Abram Fuller.

Stolen black portmanteau, now recovered. Holding for return by first available boat. Will advise.

Abram Fuller knew from this message that Leah had been found and rescued, but that it was too dangerous for her to travel the usual way, hidden among the cargo on one of his wagons. Instead she was to be rowed across the Niagara River. He waited for the message that told him which dark night had been chosen and where he should meet her on the Canadian side of the river.

Because the law in the United States was on the side of the slave owners, abolitionists depended on surprise or stealth to stage their daring rescues. Underground Railroad workers knew that once slave catchers captured a runaway, they usually telegraphed the owner, then looked for a safe place to keep their captive until the owner arrived. This gave abolitionists a few days to put their plans into action.

Just such a delay saved a fugitive slave named Patrick Snead. He had escaped to Canada but made the mistake of working in a hotel on the American side of Niagara Falls. One day a telegram arrived from his former owner ordering the local sheriff to arrest him. Even though the other waiters tried to defend him, Snead was dragged off to jail. But while the sheriff was waiting for the arrest warrant to be sworn out, Snead was spirited out of jail and across the river to Canada.

Patrick Snead was one of the lucky ones. Most captured slaves were returned to angry owners who made their lives much harsher than before.

Cornhusk Doll

The doll that Eliza left for Johanna was made from cornhusks, one of the few materials available to slave mothers like Leah Jackson. Slaves also made dolls from corn cobs, straw, twigs, nuts and dried apples, then dressed them in scraps of cloth. You can make your own cornhusk doll like Eliza's.

You'll need:
- 10 to 15 cornhusks (from the cob or a craft store)
- scissors
- newspapers
- 1 L (4 c.) warm water
- 10 mL (2 tsp.) glycerine
- a towel
- 2 pipe cleaners, each 10 cm (4 in.) long
- 2 cm (¾ in.) plastic foam ball (or crumpled paper wrapped in tape)
- strong thread
- felt markers
- fabric
- a sewing pin

1. For husks straight from the cob, trim off the bottom ends so that the husks lie flat. Dry them between layers of newspapers for about a week. For husks from a craft store, start at Step 2.

2. Soak the husks overnight in warm water mixed with glycerine. Blot them on a towel to soak up the excess water.

3. Push a pipe cleaner into the foam ball. Fold a piece of cornhusk 13 cm (5 in.) long over the ball. Place a second husk at a right angle to the first one and fold it down. Shape the husks around the ball to form the head. Wind thread several times around the neck and tie tightly.

4. Cut a strip of husk 2.5 cm x 10 cm (1 in. x 4 in.). Lay the other pipe cleaner on it lengthwise and roll up as tightly as possible. Tie thread near each end to make the wrists.

5. Lay the arm piece across the body piece below the head. Wind thread over and under the arms several times in a figure-eight pattern, then tie tightly.

6. Cut two strips of husk 4 cm x 13 cm (1 1/2 in. x 5 in.). Fold lengthwise to make strips. Crisscross the strips over the shoulders and down to the waist. Tie tightly around the waist with several turns of thread.

7. Bend the arms up beside the head. Overlap five or six husks around the waist with the wide ends pointing up. Wrap ten turns of thread tightly around the waist and tie. Fold the overlapping husks down one at a time to form a skirt. Trim it evenly at the bottom. Bend the arms down.

8. Use markers to make a face.

9. Cut a square of fabric 7.5 cm x 7.5 cm (3 in. x 3 in.). Fold it into a triangle to make a head scarf. Cross the ends under the chin and tie them behind the neck. To make an apron, cut a piece 2.5 cm x 4 cm (1 in. x 1 1/2 in.). Wrap it around the waist and use a pin to hold it in place at the back.

FINDING WORK

When Leah Jackson arrived in Toronto, she needed to find work to support her family. Leah had a number of skills that would help her. She was an expert seamstress, a good cook and a laundress. Even so, paid work was hard to come by in a country full of immigrants recently arrived from Britain and Europe. Many newcomers were scrambling for few jobs. But people who had the bravery to escape from cruel owners and the perseverance to find their way through unknown territory were not easily discouraged.

Unskilled women took in laundry, did mending, or became maids in large houses. Men who had few skills worked for the many hotels opening up. Others earned their first wages as laborers on the new steam railroad, laying track, or carrying luggage.

Railroad laborers

Shoemaker

Waiter

Washerwomen

Once they had saved enough money, some ex-slaves went into business for themselves. T.F. Cary and R.B. Richards opened the first icehouse in Toronto, cutting ice from the mill ponds in winter, storing it in sawdust, and delivering it daily by wagon in the warmer months to customers in and around the city. Another ex-slave, Thornton Blackburn, noting that Toronto was large and often muddy, bought a horse and carriage and started the city's first taxi service. Others opened shops and became barbers, seamstresses, shoemakers or bakers, using skills learned in their slave days.

Not all former slaves went to the cities. Some took up land north and west of Toronto. There they cleared the bush and established farms. Many descendants of former slaves still live in the Chatham area.

Vendors

Seamstresses

Taxi driver

LEARNING TO BE FREE

Ben had been a field hand on the plantation, so he had fewer skills than his mother and sister, but he was keen to learn. Like other escaped slaves, Ben knew that learning to read and write was an important step in finding work and settling down. He also wanted to learn practical skills, so he applied to the school at Dawn, near Chatham, Canada West (now Ontario).

Josiah Henson, an escaped slave, felt that ex-slaves needed schools not only to teach them how to read and write, but also how to buy and farm land. He joined with a group of Quakers and Unitarians concerned about the welfare of black refugees and built a school, sawmill and gristmill. By attending the school, working in the mills and farming the land, the students learned the skills they needed. The Dawn school lasted from 1844 to 1868.

A more successful school, The Elgin Settlement near Chatham, was started by William King, a Presbyterian minister. King felt that ex-slaves needed three things: land, schools and churches. He started by buying 3600 ha (8900 acres) of land, which he divided into farms of 20 ha (50 acres) each. Ex-slaves could buy land cheaply as long as they agreed to build a cabin and begin clearing the land and planting crops. Those who had no money were encouraged to work for the railroads until they had earned the $12.50 for the first payment.

King also oversaw the building of a combination church and school, which was open to everyone. Over the next 15 years, the school attracted an equal number of black and white students. By 1865, more than 700 students had attended the school, many of whom went on to university and became community leaders. Later, the school merged with other public schools to become the local district school.

MARY ANN SHADD

Some people felt that blacks and whites should have separate schools. Not teacher and journalist Mary Ann Shadd. She was against any form of segregation.

Mary Ann Shadd was born into a free black family in Delaware. Her family were strong abolitionists who helped many slaves on their flight north. In this atmosphere, she learned to care about the plight of the unfortunate and to speak her mind.

In 1850, Mary Ann went to Windsor, Canada West (now Ontario), to set up a school for escaped slaves. Unlike the school at Dawn, hers was integrated. She believed that only by educating black children and white children together would the two groups learn to treat each other as equals.

Some white people in the area disagreed. Many refused to let their children attend school with black students. In an attempt to change these attitudes, Mary Ann established a newspaper, *The Provincial Freeman*. But the double load of teaching and writing exhausted her, and after only two years she had to close the school. The newspaper survived and was moved to Toronto, where many people were strongly abolitionist and supported her ideas. *The Provincial Freeman* lasted for about six years and was a strong and influential voice for the black community.

In 1864, while the Civil War still raged, Mary Ann was asked to return to the United States to help recruit black soldiers for the Union army. After the war, she moved to Washington, D.C., where she taught school during the day and attended law school at Howard University at night. As a lawyer, she fought for many causes, including the right of women to vote. This remarkable woman achieved two notable firsts: she was the first black woman in North America to establish and run a newspaper, and the first woman to study for a law degree from an American university.

113

FREEDOM FOR ALL

On January 1, 1863, President Abraham Lincoln signed the Emancipation Proclamation, declaring all slaves free. At last escaped slaves in the northern States and Canada were safe from abduction by slave catchers.

The news of emancipation unsettled many of the refugees just learning to live in Canada. Most had left relatives and friends in the South. Although they had run from the whips of their owners and the tracking dogs of the slave hunters, they were still attached to the places where they had been born. Once the Civil War ended, hundreds decided to return to their birthplaces. Sadly, some faced harsh treatment and violence there.

But others stayed in Canada. They had built houses, established businesses and started families. They had put down roots. Difficult though it was to adjust to the colder climate and disappointing as it was to find that prejudice still existed, their new country was now home. Today, nearly a century and a half later, the descendants of ex-slaves are fifth and sixth generation Canadians with a long history of helping to build the country.

GLOSSARY

abolitionist — a person who believed in, and worked toward, the freeing of the slaves

American Civil War — a war (1861-65) between the northern and southern states that brought about the abolition of slavery

auction block — a platform on which slaves stood to be offered for sale

bondage — the institution of slavery

code — a system of words, sounds or symbols used to communicate secretly

emancipation — freedom from bondage

flog — to beat with a stick or a whip

free states — states that had proclaimed slavery illegal. (See pages 18-19.)

fugitive slave — a runaway slave

manacles — heavy iron bands that fastened around the wrists and were joined by a short iron chain to restrict movement

manumission — a legal release from slavery. Some owners left instructions in their wills that their slaves were to be freed or manumitted.

massa — the pronunciation some southerners gave to the word "master"

overseer — a person who directed the work of the field slaves

patrollers — men mounted on horseback who guarded southern roads against escaping slaves

plantation — a very large farm

Promised Land — a code name for Canada taken from the story of the Israelites' escape from Egypt in the Bible

safe house — a hiding place for escaped slaves

slave — a person held in servitude as the property of another

slave auction — a place where slaves were offered for sale

slave catcher — a person who earned his living by tracking escaped slaves, capturing them and returning them to their owners for the reward money

spirituals — deeply emotional songs based on Bible stories. They were created by slaves to give them comfort and hope.

BIBLIOGRAPHY

Every escaped slave had a unique story to tell. Here are more stories of the Underground Railroad.

Novels and Biographies

Lasky, Kathryn. *True North: A Novel of the Underground Railroad*. The Blue Sky Press/Scholastic, 1996

Lyons, Mary E. *Letters from a Slave Girl: The Story of Harriet Jacobs*. Charles Scribner's Sons, 1992

McCurdy, Michael. *Escape From Slavery: The Boyhood of Frederick Douglass in His Own Words*. Alfred A. Knopf, 1994

Paterson, Katherine. *Jip: His Story*. Lodestar Books, 1996

Petry, Ann. *Harriet Tubman: Conductor on the Underground Railroad*. Harper Trophy, 1955, 1983

Smucker, Barbara. *Underground to Canada*. Puffin, 1978

Picture Books for All Ages

Bryan, Ashley. *All Day, All Night: A Child's First Book of African-American Spirituals*. Atheneum, 1991

Edwards, Pamela Duncan (illus. Henry Cole). *Barefoot: Escape on the Underground Railroad*. HarperCollins, 1997

Johnston, Tony. *The Wagon*. Tambourine Books, 1996

McKissock, Patricia. *Christmas in the Big House, Christmas in the Quarters*. Scholastic, 1994

Winter, Jeanette. *Follow the Drinking Gourd*. Alfred A. Knopf, 1988

Histories

Gorrell, Gena K. *North Star to Freedom: The Story of the Underground Railroad*. Stoddart, 1996

Hamilton, Virginia. *Many Thousand Gone*. Knopf/Random House, 1993

INDEX

A
abolitionists, 16, 42-43, 57, 71, 89, 107
activities
  cornhusk doll, 108-109
  follow the North Star, 41
  gingerbread cookies, 38-39
  lantern-making, 60-61
  songs, 92-93
  storytelling, 74-75
American Civil War, 113, 114
anti-slavery meetings, 71
Anti-Slavery Society of Canada, 42
See also abolitionists
Auburn, New York, 21
auctions, slave, 40-41, 92

B
Baby, Charles, 88
Belleville, Ontario, 91
Bible stories, 23, 92
Big Dipper. *See* North Star
Blackburn, Thornton, 111
Brer Rabbit, 72-73
Brown, Henry, 58

C
Cary, T. F., 111
Chatham, Ontario, 88, 111, 112
Cincinnati, Ohio, 43
codes, 17, 20-21, 106
Coffin, Levi and Catherine, 43
cotton, 56
cotton gins, 56
Craft, Ellen and William, 59

D
Davids, Tice, 16
Dawn Institute, 112
Detroit River, 88
dolls, 108-109
Douglass, Frederick, 71

E
education, slaves, 70, 71, 112-113
Emancipation Proclamation, 42, 114
escapes, slave, 58-59, 88-89, 107

F
Fugitive Slave law, 17, 42

G
gingerbread cookies, 38-39

H
Henson, Josiah, 112

K
King, William, 112

L
lanterns, 60-61
Lincoln, Abraham, 114

M
manumission, 57
Mississippi River, 54
Moses, 20, 21, 23, 93
music, 92-93
  as code, 17
  as comfort, 55
  as defiance, 41
  passing on history, 72

N
New York City, 71
Newport, Indiana, 43
newspapers, 71, 113
Niagara Falls, New York, 107
Niagara River, 106
North Star, 41

P
Philadelphia, Pennsylvania, 21, 58
plantations, 34-35, 54-55
  crops, 23, 34, 54
  food, 36, 38-39
  laundry, 37
  sewing, 37
Promised Land, 20, 42, 92

Q
Quakers. *See* Society of Friends

R
reading, 70, 72, 112
rewards for slaves, 20, 89
  posters, 89
Richards, R.B., 111
Richmond, Virginia, 58
Rochester, New York, 71
Ross, Alexander, 91

S
safe houses, 16, 57
schools, 112, 113
sewing machines, 37
Shadd, Mary Ann, 88, 113
signals
  code words, 17
  drums, 93
  lantern, 60, 57
  music, 17
  owl hoot, 21
Simcoe, John Graves, 42
slave catchers, 17, 88-89, 106
slaves
  auctions, 40-41
  captured in Africa, 22
  education of, 70, 71, 112-113
  escapes, 58-59, 88-89, 107

  food, 54-55
  freed, 57
  in Canada, 42
  posters about, 89
  rewards for, 20, 89
  work after escape, 110-111
  work on plantations, 23, 36-37, 40, 54-55
Snead, Patrick, 107
Society of Friends (Quakers), 42, 59
spirituals (songs), 92-93
St. Catharines, Ontario, 4, 16, 21, 71, 89
storytelling, 72-73, 74-75
Stowe, Harriet Beecher, 43, 91
swamp ghosts, 58

T
telegraph, 106
The *North Star*, 71
The Provincial Freeman, 113
Toronto, Ontario, 88, 89, 110, 111, 113
Tubman, Harriet, 20-21

U
Uncle Tom's Cabin, 43, 91
Underground Railroad, 4, 16, 57, 106-107
  routes, 18-19

V
vote, right to, 71

W
Whitney, Eli, 56
Windsor, Ontario, 59, 88, 113
writing, 70, 72, 112